Baby Cakes

The Cupcake Club

Sheryl Berk and Carrie Berk

sourcebooks
jabberwocky

Published by Sourcebooks Jabberwocky, an imprint of Sourcebooks, Inc.
P.O. Box 4410, Naperville, Illinois 60567-4410
(630) 961-3900
Fax: (630) 961-2168
www.jabberwockykids.com

Library of Congress Cataloging-in-Publication data is on file with the pub-
lisher.

Source of Production: Versa Press, East Peoria, Illinois, USA
Date of Production: January 2014
Run Number: 5000461

Printed and bound in the United States of America.
VP 10 9 8 7 6 5 4 3 2 1

To Our Sweet Mama Chickie—
you're always in our hearts.

The Proud, the Free... the Chicopee!

Kylie Carson climbed on the camp bus and took a seat in a row by herself. She was excited about her first summer at sleepaway camp, but also nervous. She'd never been away from home for six weeks.

"You'll love Camp Chicopee," her dad insisted. "Your old man went there a few years back, and I had a blast!"

"A few years?" Her mom chuckled. "Try thirty years ago!"

"Who's counting?" her father replied. "Besides, I looked at the website and everything looks exactly the same. Right down to the giant rooster sculpture on the front lawn."

He turned to Kylie and patted her on the back. "Just be your smiley Kylie self, and you'll make tons of new friends."

It hadn't been easy for Kylie to make friends at Blakely Elementary when she was a new student in third grade. What she did make easily were enemies, namely one Meredith Mitchell who still couldn't stand her. But now, two years later, she had three fabulous BFFs: Lexi Poole, Jenna Medina, and Sadie Harris. Together, they'd formed Peace, Love, and Cupcakes, a cupcake club that had turned into a booming baking business. She was sad to leave the girls behind for the summer, but the club's advisor, Juliette Dubois, thought it would be good for all the girls to take some time off, relax, and regroup.

So while Lexi went to NYC to study art, Jenna went to Ecuador to visit her grandma, and Sadie headed to basketball camp in North Carolina, Kylie was on her way to Camp Chicopee in Massachusetts.

"Is this seat taken?" a voice interrupted her thoughts. A girl with strawberry blond hair pulled back in two loose braids smiled at her. "If I don't sit in the front of the bus, I get carsick."

Kylie wrinkled her nose. "You won't puke on me, will you?"

The girl shook her head. "Nah. I only puke at midnight when there's a full moon…"

Kylie giggled. "Kind of like a werewolf without the hair and claws?"

The girl raised the sleeve on her hoodie. "Yup. Fur-free…for now!" She gave an evil, mad-scientist chuckle and settled into the seat next to Kylie.

"I'm Delaney Noonan," the girl said. Kylie glanced out the window. A mom and dad were holding up a sign that read, "We love you, Delaney! XOXO!"

"I guess those are your parents," Kylie said, pointing. "The ones in the Camp Chicopee baseball hats?"

Delaney covered her eyes with her hand. "So embarrassing!"

"Not any more than mine!" Kylie motioned at her parents who were waving wildly at the bus window and blowing kisses. Her dad was wearing his old Chicopee T-shirt that he had dug out of a trunk in the attic. Instead of white, it was now a strange yellow-brown, but you could still see the rooster mascot and the camp slogan, "Proud, Free, Chicopee!" across the chest. "I'm Kylie, by the way," she said.

"Nice to meet you, Kylie By-the-Way," Delaney joked. "That's an interesting last name."

Kylie rolled her eyes. Delaney reminded her of her friend Jenna. She was always making jokes.

"What cabin are you in?" Delaney asked. "I'm in G2."

"G2? Me too!" Kylie answered. "Cool!"

That was how their friendship began.

Delaney remembered how she and Kylie had talked all the way on the two-hour bus ride to camp. They had so much in common! Delaney love, love, loved vampire movies—especially *Twilight* and *Dracula*. The spookier, the better! And Kylie knew even more about them than she did.

"Did you know that there have been more than two hundred movies made with Dracula in them?" she asked Delaney.

"Wow. That's a ton!" Delaney gasped. "Have you seen them all?"

Kylie thought hard. "Well, not all—but a lot. I'm checking them off as I go along."

"And did you know there are about a gazillion songs with monster names in the title?" Delaney pointed out. "I'm not even counting Lady Gaga's album. I'm talking about 'Monster Mash,' 'Werewolves of London,' 'Zombie Dance'…"

Kylie was wowed. "I don't think I've ever met anyone who could name monster music," she said.

"And I don't think I ever met anyone who knew how to make fake blood out of corn syrup!" Delaney replied.

"Oh, I am a master at it," Kylie bragged. "What's really cool is how you can make it taste good so you can use it to fill Halloween cupcakes. You take a bite and the blood oozes out."

Delaney made a face. "Oh, that is disgusting. I have *got* to try it!" They both laughed.

They decided that at the first marshmallow roast, when everyone gathered around the campfire at night to tell ghost stories, their vampire tale would be the best and the creepiest in all of Camp Chicopee.

2

Cupcakes That Go Bump in the Night

The Chicopee campfire cookout was the highlight of the summer. Besides the yummy burgers, hot dogs, and roasted s'mores, everyone looked forward to the spooky tales campers and counselors told around the fire.

Kylie and Delaney's senior counselor, Kay, was up first. "On a night just like this one, around a campfire just like this one, a group of kids heard a noise echo in the distance."

"What was the noise?" asked Skylar, one of the G2 cabinmates.

"It sounded like this…" Kay cupped her hand over her mouth and made a strange, clucking sound.

"What is that?" Delaney asked. "Sounds like a chicken laying an egg."

"Shh!" Skylar hushed her. "This is getting good!"

Kay continued. "The noise came closer…and closer…

and closer, until the kids could feel a hot breath on the back of their necks."

Skylar screamed. "I feel it! I feel it!"

"All I feel is Skylar's clammy hand grabbing me," Delaney said, giving her a shove. "Seriously? This is not scary."

"Click…tap-tap-tap. Click…tap-tap-tap," Kay said. "The strange sound came closer and closer until…"

Gabby and Rhiannon, the two other G2 counselors, ran out from the woods dressed in frilly skirts, dancing and clicking castanets in their hands.

Kylie and Delaney looked at each other. "And this is supposed to scare us?" Delaney sighed. "Amateurs." She turned to Kylie. "Let's show 'em how it's done."

"It was a cool, dark night in June…" Kylie began. "A lone figure made his way through the bushes in search of something to satisfy his tremendous hunger."

Delaney continued: "He sniffed the air, until his nose caught the scent of something so delectable that nothing could prevent him from taking a bite."

The campers leaned in closer. "What did he bite?" one girl in G3 asked.

Delaney leaned in closer and whispered, "It was something warm…and sticky!"

"EEEK!" the campers squealed. "Was it blood? Did he bite someone's neck?"

Delaney and Kylie looked at each other and smiled. "Oh, no…not a person or even an animal," Kylie added. "It was…"

"What? What?" Skylar yelled. "Tell us! I can't stand the suspense!"

Delaney and Kylie shouted together: *A cupcake!*

The campers groaned and threw marshmallows at them. Delaney was delighted—even if her hair was sticky when she went to bed that night. She loved having an audience hang on her every word.

"What do you want to be when you grow up?" Kylie asked her when they were lying awake in their bunks.

"Dunno. Maybe a singer like Katy Perry or Lady Gaga."

Kylie laughed. "I think you'd look great in Gaga's Kermit the Frog coat!"

"Or maybe a stand-up comedian. My dad says I'm a natural," Delaney added. "I always crack him up. How about you? Do you want to run a cupcake bakery?"

Kylie nodded. "I'd love to expand our business around the world. Can't you just see a Peace, Love, and Cupcakes in Paris…or London…or Australia?"

"You can come to my sold-out stadium tour if I can get a red velvet cupcake anywhere I go," Delaney said. "Filled with fake blood, of course." She reached down from the top bunk so they could shake hands on it.

✮ ☮ ✮

So that's how Kylie ended up asking Delaney to join the cupcake club. At first, her fellow PLCers didn't like the idea—especially Lexi, who thought four members were enough. But Delaney had not only proved that she could bake and frost like a pro, but also that she was a lot of fun to have around.

"Check this out!" she said, piping a red rose on her nose. "I'm a cupcake clown!"

She also believed that baking needed a sound track. "What shall we play today?" she asked as Sadie preheated the oven to 350 degrees. "I'm kind of in a pop mood…but I could definitely go for an oldie but goodie."

She selected a song on her MP3 player and "Candy Girl" by The Archies filled Kylie's kitchen.

"Sugar, sugar!" Delaney jumped up on a chair and crooned into a wooden spoon. "Oh, honey, honey!"

Soon, they were all dancing around and tossing flour in each other's hair.

"Delaney, what would we do without you?" Sadie laughed, trying to catch her breath.

"Less laundry?" Lexi teased, wiping flour off her jeans. "But it's true. Even when we have a crazy, impossible deadline, you make it seem fun and doable." Delaney smiled and took a bow.

Her dad said "fun" was her middle name. (It was really Miriam after her great-granny.) And her mom compared her to a duck: "Water and problems just roll right off your back."

Delaney guessed that was why her parents decided she'd take the news well. They were having her favorite breakfast one Sunday morning—a scrambled-egg and sausage wafflewich—when her mom put down her coffee cup and cleared her throat.

"Laney," she began. "Daddy and I have something very exciting to share with you. A really big surprise."

Delaney looked up from her plate. "We're going to Disneyland?" she guessed. "Awesome!"

"No, honey," her father added. "It's much bigger than that."

Delaney tried to wrap her brain around what could be better than a surprise vacation to an amusement park. "Is it seats to the Katy Perry concert in May? OMG! I was dying to go!"

11

"No, no." Her mom looked anxiously at her dad. "It's not a concert either."

"Wait! Wait! Is it a new cell phone? OMG, Kylie will be so jealous!"

Delaney looked at both their faces and tried to read them. "What could be bigger than a concert or a vacation or the new iPhone?" she asked. "I give up! What's the surprise?"

Her mother took her hand and held it tight. "Honey, it's the best, biggest surprise ever." She took a deep breath: "We're having a baby!"

Delaney's mouth hung wide open. For once, she couldn't think of anything funny to say. "A baby?" she gasped. "Is this a joke?"

"Afraid not," her dad replied, ruffling his hair. "We thought you'd be excited."

"I am. I think. It's just that babies, they're small. And they pee and poop, like all the time. And they cry... really loudly."

"You forgot the spitting-up part," her mom added. "Yes, they do all those things. Which is why your little brother or sister will be so lucky to have you to help."

"But I don't know how to change diapers," Delaney

said. "And what about burping? How do you even burp a little baby?" She pushed her chair away from the table.

"Where are you going?" her mom asked.

Delaney looked very serious, more serious than she had ever looked in her entire life. "I have a lot of studying to do," she said.

She raced to her bedroom, speed-dialed Kylie, and didn't even wait for her to say hello.

"Kyles, remember how you taught me the crawl and butterfly stroke at Camp Chicopee in one day?" she asked.

"Um, yeah," Kylie replied. "We needed to win the swim relay against Skylar and Ally, and all you could do was doggy paddle."

"Right! Well, I only have a few months to learn how to be a big sister, and I need all the help I can get!"

3

Big Sis in Training

Kylie called an emergency meeting of Peace, Love, and Cupcakes the next day after school at her house. The girls had no idea what the reason was; they assumed it was some kind of cupcake calamity, as usual.

"So, what did you sign us up for this time?" Jenna smirked. "A thousand cupcakes shaped like poodles? A replica of the Statue of Liberty made out of minis?" As the club's official taste tester, she knew she had to get her taste buds prepared.

Kylie shook her head. "No, there are actually no cupcakes involved." She looked at Delaney. "Do you want to fill them in?"

Delaney took a deep breath and blurted it out. "My mom is having a baby!"

Lexi squealed. "That's awesome! Congratulations! I have always wanted to make little babies out of fondant." It was just like Lexi to be thinking about cupcake decorating at a time like this. She was an incredible artist who'd taught Delaney everything she knew about sculpting and piping.

"You're going to be a big sis!" Sadie chimed in. "I'm jealous. I'm always the youngest in my family." Although Sadie had two big brothers, she was quite the athlete herself—not to mention a whiz with a whisk.

"*Buena suerte*…good luck!" Jenna added. "I have two little brothers, and they are a handful!"

Delaney sighed dramatically. "Tell me about it! I have no clue how to be a big sister. I don't even know what you do with this!" She held up a diaper.

Lexi giggled. "Um, you put it on the baby's butt."

"I know what you do with it," Delaney explained. "I just don't know *how*. Or which way. Or what all this sticky tape is for."

Jenna grabbed the diaper out of her hands. "Kylie, give me that sack of flour."

Kylie took the flour off the kitchen counter and handed it to her.

"Okay, I changed a gazillion of my brothers' diapers when they were babies…" Jenna boasted. With a few quick folds, the diaper was wrapped snuggly around the flour.

She picked it up, pretending to rock it in her arms. "There you go, bambino," she joked. "Doesn't that feel better?"

Sadie laughed. "Hey, pass the baby over here. I'm open!"

The diaper-clad flour flew through the air. Sadie caught it, then pretended to burp it on her shoulder. "Make burpsie, baby," she cooed before letting loose a loud burp.

"Ugh!" Delaney groaned. "Cut it out! This isn't funny!"

Lexi looked puzzled. "Delaney, what happened to your sense of humor?"

Kylie stepped in to defend her friend. "I think Delaney is feeling a little nervous about the new baby."

"A *little* nervous?" Delaney huffed. "Try a lot nervous. I know you all think I'm a practical joker and the club clown…"

Jenna nodded. "And we would be right. You're a riot!"

"Well, I can't be—not anymore," Delaney replied. "My little brother or sister is going to need me to be responsible. So that's it. From now on, I'm Miss Serious."

Kylie raised an eyebrow. "You really want us to help you be serious?" In all the time she had known Delaney, "serious" had never even been in her friend's vocabulary.

"Absolutely," Delaney insisted. She sat up perfectly straight on the kitchen stool and crossed her arms over her chest. "No more joking, no more singing into mixing spoons, no more dancing on the kitchen counter."

Sadie smiled. "You left out sprinkling your hair with white flour and pretending to be Ludwig van Beethoven."

"Oh, that was a classic," Jenna chimed in. "Dum-dum-dum-dum…" She pretended to play the kitchen counter like a piano.

Delaney didn't crack a smile. She didn't seem amused at all. "No more."

"Well, as your fellow cupcake clubbers, we will of course respect your wishes," Kylie said. "But I will miss the old Delaney who sang 'La Bamba' using whisks for maracas."

"Oh! What about the time you painted your face with Lexi's green tea frosting and cackled like the Wicked Witch?" Sadie recalled. "'I'll get you, my pretty…and your little cupcake too!'"

Delaney didn't flinch. "No. There'll be none of that either."

Kylie could tell her friend meant business. This was important to her—the most important thing she had ever done in her life. "Okay, Delaney. We will do our very best to help you be serious."

"This won't be easy," Jenna added. "It requires a complete personality transplant."

Delaney was ready for it. Her parents were depending on her. Her new baby brother or sister needed her. "I can take it."

☆ ☮ ☆

Kylie suggested they try out a new recipe in the kitchen— and try out Delaney's new work routine. "I had this crazy idea to do brunch cupcakes that look like eggs sunny-side up," she said.

"Ooh!" Lexi cried. "Love it! I could use yellow fondant for the yolks."

"What flavor should the cake be?" Jenna asked. "Maybe maple syrup? French toast?"

"Wheat germ!" Sadie shouted. "I love wheat germ for breakfast! It's so healthy for you!"

Jenna made a face. "Wheat germ? Seriously, Sadie, you scare me sometimes!"

Kylie looked at Delaney. "Do you want to add anything?"

Delaney thought hard. What she wanted to do was make a joke about eggs—something that would "crack" everyone up. Instead, she said, "Sounds fine. Let's be careful not to burn ourselves on the oven."

The girls all stared. "Seriously? You have nothing more

egg-citing to say?" Jenna asked. "How about cracking an egg on your head like you did when we made the Easter egg cupcakes?"

Delaney ignored her, tied the apron around her waist, and went to get the ingredients they needed out of the kitchen cupboards.

"I'm not sure I love the new Delaney," Sadie whispered to Kylie. "She's kind of a sourpuss."

"She's just trying her best," Kylie said. "We're her friends and we have to stick by her."

The kitchen was silent, except for the sound of the mixer beating the batter. Kylie's mom came in to investigate.

"It's too quiet in here. Are you girls up to something?" Mrs. Carson asked.

"Nope," Kylie assured her. "Just bakin'."

"No singing? No dancing? No Katy Perry blasting?" her mom said.

All eyes turned to Delaney. She was focused on measuring out exactly one teaspoon of vanilla for the icing.

"Okay," Mrs. Carson said. "Have fun."

"Or not," Jenna muttered under her breath. "This is the most boring baking I have ever done."

"She does have a point," Lexi whispered to Kylie. "Part

of what makes PLC so great is how we all love to be together and have fun making cupcakes. "

"I feel like I'm grounded," Sadie said.

Jenna decided it was time to take matters into her own hands. She scooped a dollop of frosting out of Lexi's bowl and smudged it right on Delaney's nose. "What do you have to say about *that*?" she teased.

Delaney stood frozen in place. If this was last week, she would have smudged more frosting on her face and pretended to be Santa Claus…or Rip Van Winkle…or a giant marshmallow man. But it was today, and she had promised herself it was time to turn over a new leaf.

She reached for a napkin on the counter and gingerly wiped the icing off.

"Ugh!" Jenna cried. "You are just no fun!"

Delaney didn't want to disappoint her friends, but that's how things had to be from now on.

4

A Tangled Web

The next morning at Weber Day School, Delaney's English teacher, Ms. Kutchen, announced the class would be putting on a musical for the school's mini-term. Mini-term was always a lot of fun: a whole month of creative, exciting ways to learn subjects. Ms. Kutchen wanted to take a book of literature they were going to read in class and whip it into a performance worthy of a Broadway stage.

Delaney loved musicals! She hoped her teacher had chosen one of her favorites, *Matilda*, since it was based on the book by Roald Dahl. It was hard to sit quietly in her seat and contain her excitement. But this was the new Delaney—the one who acted calm, cool, and mature. Even though it was killing her!

"I've chosen one of my favorite books to inspire our musical," her teacher said. "And I've already assigned you all parts."

Olivia Isaacman's hand shot up. "No auditions?"

"No, no auditions," Ms. Kutchen replied. "There will be a great part for everyone."

She handed Delaney a pink headband with two fluffy ears attached. "I think you'll be very happy with your role," her teacher said, smiling.

"What's this?" Delaney asked. She didn't think there were any pig ears in *Matilda*.

"It's your costume. You're Wilbur the Pig in *Charlotte's Web*!"

The classroom erupted in laughter as Ms. Kutchen walked around the room, handing out scripts and assigning kids their roles. Delaney felt sick to her stomach. How could she be taken seriously wearing pig ears and a snout?

"Awesome! Or should I say 'oink-some'?" Harrison Holt teased.

"You are going to be hilarious!" her friend Sophie Spivac whispered. "You get to roll around in the mud!"

Delaney frowned. "Who are you playing?" she asked. Sophie was an amazing singer and took voice lessons after school.

Sophie looked down at her script. On the top, Ms. Kutchen had written "Charlotte."

"I guess we'll be besties in the play too?" Sophie smiled.

"That's so not fair!" Delaney couldn't hold back her feelings anymore and jumped up out of her seat. "You get the serious part! You get to wear black and spin a web and even die at the end!"

Ms. Kutchen looked shocked and confused by her outburst. "Delaney, I thought you'd be thrilled to play Wilbur."

"How can I be serious…wearing these?" Delaney threw the pink pig ears on the ground and ran out of the room in tears.

☆ ☮ ☆

No matter how hard she tried, no one thought of her as anything more than a joke. Not her friends. Not her English teacher. She sat down in the corner of the hallway by her locker and buried her head in her hands.

"Penny for your thoughts," said a voice. It was Ms. Roveen, the school guidance counselor.

"I don't wanna talk about it," Delaney replied.

"It must be something very serious then," Ms. Roveen said.

"That's just it! It's not serious! Nothing I do is serious! I'm a big joke."

Ms. Roveen sat down beside her. "Now you've lost me. A joke has you this upset?"

"Everyone thinks I'm a joke," Delaney answered. "I have to wear pig ears. And roll around in mud. And I don't even know how to change a diaper!"

"Do pigs change diapers?" Ms. Roveen teased. "Now that's news to me."

"You see?" Delaney sighed. "Even you think I'm a joke!"

"I don't think you're a joke, Delaney," Ms. Roveen said, trying to calm her. "I made a joke to try and cheer you up. There's nothing wrong with having a sense of humor."

"There is when you have to be a big sister," Delaney said quietly. "My mom's having a baby—and I don't know anything about having a little sister or brother."

"Ah, so that's the issue! You're going to be a big sister, and you think you need to change who you are to be a good one."

Finally! Someone understood! "Exactly!" Delaney replied.

"I think I have a good solution for you," Ms. Roveen said. "I'll call your mom and make sure she's cool with it, but I'd like you to come to my house today after school."

Delaney looked puzzled. "What for?"

Ms. Roveen smiled. "To babysit, of course!"

5

Silly Milly

When Delaney rang Ms. Roveen's bell, the door creaked open slowly, and a tiny pair of blue eyes peeked out at her. She could see it was a toddler—there were pink princess slippers poking out as well.

"Um, hi?" Delaney said, trying to be very mature. "I'm Delaney. I'm the babysitter."

"I Milly!" said a little voice. "You come play?"

Just then, Ms. Roveen opened the door. "Millicent McKenzie, what did Mommy tell you about opening the door to strangers?" She sighed. "She's very excited to see you."

"It's Dee-Lay-Neeeeeee!" the little girl sang. She had wavy blond curls—just like Ms. Roveen—and dimples when she smiled.

"Tell Delaney how old you are," her mother instructed.

Milly held up two chubby fingers. "I two! I big girl!"

"You are a big girl," Ms. Roveen said, scooping her up in her arms. "She'll be two in a month. And you're going to be a big girl while Mommy does some work. Delaney is going to take care of you."

"I am? I mean, by myself?" Delaney felt her stomach twitch. "I'm not sure I really know how…"

"There's not much to it." Ms. Roveen ushered her inside. "These are Milly's sippy cup and her snacks. She loves Cheerios and applesauce. And this is her playroom with all her toys. She wears pull-up diapers, so you might have to change her…"

Milly squiggled free from her mom's arms and raced over to get a pink wand.

"This my magic wand!" She giggled. "Bibby boo! Bibby boo!"

"She means 'Bibbidi-Bobbidi-Boo,'" Ms. Roveen whispered. "She's obsessed with Cinderella."

Delaney nodded, trying to remember all the details: sippy cup, Cheerios, bibby boo…and what exactly was a pull-up?

"Okay, I'm off to do my work upstairs. You just hang out here with Milly for an hour, and I'll see you later."

"Wait!" Delaney called after her. "What if I mess up? What if Milly doesn't like me?"

Ms. Roveen smiled. "Of course she'll like you, Delaney. Just be yourself." She waved to Milly. "Have fun! Bye, girls!"

Before Delaney could protest any further, she felt a little hand tugging on her pant leg.

"I Cindyrella and you Pwince Arming," Milly insisted.

"Um, okay," Delaney said. "What do you want me to do?"

"You Pwince Arming!" Milly stamped her foot.

"I get it. I'm Prince Charming. What does Prince Charming do?"

Milly's cheeks flushed. She squinted her eyes and wrinkled her nose. *"I want Mama!"* she howled and began to cry.

"Wait! No! Just a sec! Don't cry!" Delaney begged her. She took off her sneaker. "Cindyrella! I have your glass slipper."

Milly only wailed harder: *"Mama! Mama! Mama!"*

Think! Delaney told herself. What would Prince Charming do?

"Would Cindyrella like to go to the ball with Pwince Arming?" she asked the screaming toddler.

Milly's tears suddenly stopped. "I go ball. I dance." She sniffled.

"Yes! Yes! We can dance! And we can have a tea party! And get all dressed up in pwincess, I mean, princess dresses!"

"Ooooh!" Milly squealed. "I like pwincess dress."

Delaney had no idea where she was going to find a princess dress on such short notice. She looked in the hall coat closet, hoping to find one hanging in there. But Milly was losing patience.

"I want my pwincess dress!" she said, stamping her feet.

Delaney opened the linen closet in the hall and rummaged through it. Just then, an idea came to her. She grabbed a pink towel and tied it around the child's waist. Then she grabbed a red towel and tied it around her own shoulders like a cape. "This is your beautiful princess gown," she said. "May I have this dance, Princess Milly?"

She helped Milly stand on top of her feet. "Hold on tight," she told her, as they waltzed around the room. Delaney remembered her dad doing this with her when she was little. She always loved the dizzy feeling of spinning as she clung to his knees.

"Whee!" Milly giggled in delight. "Sing me song, Pwince Arming."

It had been a very long time since Delaney had watched *Cinderella*. She couldn't think of a single song from the

Disney film—so she improvised a little Katy Perry. "I am a champion, and you're gonna hear me roar!"

"Woar! Woar!" Milly sang with her.

"Wow, you're a good singer, Princess Milly," Delaney declared. "What should we do next?"

"Tea party! Tea party!" Milly suddenly ran off to the kitchen, leaving Delaney in her dust.

Before Delaney even had a chance to search the cabinets and pour some snacks in a bowl, Milly had seized the box of Cheerios on the kitchen table and was throwing them all over the floor. She had also managed to unscrew the top of her sippy cup and was sprinkling apple juice in the air.

"It waining! It waining!" She laughed, pouring the cereal and apple juice on the tiles.

"Wait! Milly…let me help you!" Delaney raced toward her. She felt herself suddenly losing her footing, and she landed with a hard *thud* on her back on the kitchen floor.

"Deelaynee go *boom*!" Milly said. "That funny!"

Great, even a two-year-old thought she was a joke.

"Okay, Milly, let's clean up these Cheerios. They're a little slippery when wet…"

"*Nooooo!*" Milly wailed once again.

Delaney took a deep breath. "Okay, Milly. I'm in

charge here, and we're going to play a new game. It's called Cindyrella Clean Up." She found a small brush and dust pan under the sink and handed them to the little girl.

"You sweep, I mop," she said.

Milly pouted. "I no sweep." She threw herself down on the floor and went into a tantrum. *"I no sweep! I no sweep!"*

Delaney scooped the screaming toddler up in one arm and mopped with the other. She felt something wet trickling down her elbow.

"Eww! Milly, is your diaper wet?" she asked, wrinkling her nose.

"Milly go pee-pee," she replied.

Oh, boy! Delaney sighed. Where exactly did Ms. Roveen keep the diapers?

"Let's go look for some diapers," she said, carrying the child into her nursery. "Where does Mommy put them?"

"No dipee!" Milly yelled. *"I big girl! Pull-ups!"*

"Oh!" Delaney exclaimed. That's what her mom had meant. "Where does Mommy have your pull-ups?"

Milly pointed to a cabinet above the changing table. When Delaney opened it, a pile of diapers fell out and landed on her head.

"Pull-ups!" Milly suddenly said, pulling off her soggy diaper and dancing around the room.

"Okay! Let's put on a nice clean one." Delaney tried to coax her to stop jumping around. "Milly! Come back!"

Milly jumped on the bed, crawled under the changing table, and even ducked between Delaney's legs.

There was no catching her, unless…

"Milly, wanna see Pwince Arming's crown?" Delaney put the diaper on her head and grinned. "Like it?"

Milly stopped and stared…then burst into laughter. "You silly! You silly!"

Delaney scooped her up and pulled the clean diaper snuggly over her legs and bottom. "No, you're silly! Silly Milly!"

They collapsed on Milly's pink fuzzy rug, laughing and tickling each other.

Just then, Ms. Roveen walked in.

"Well, it looks like you two are getting along great!" she said.

"Mama! Deelaynee silly! I love Deelaynee!" Milly threw her arms around Delaney's neck and squeezed her tight.

Delaney smiled. Maybe she wasn't the most "serious" babysitter—but if you asked Milly, she was the most fun.

6

Surprise, Surprise

The next day, Delaney felt a little better about her ability to care for a baby brother or sister. Milly had been tough to control or predict, but at least Delaney had kept her cool and handled it. Ms. Roveen was so pleased that she'd asked Delaney to babysit any weekend she was free.

"That's great!" Kylie said when she called. "But I don't think you'll be free the weekend of the seventeenth. We have a VIP order booked, and trust me, you of all people don't wanna miss it."

Delaney tried to imagine who the VIP might be—and what the occasion was. An album release for Selena Gomez? Maybe some huge record producer's anniversary party? Or a red-carpet movie premiere in NYC?

Kylie shot down all of her guesses.

"You have to tell me! I'm going to explode if you don't!" Delaney pleaded.

"Nope. Not until everyone is together for our meeting tomorrow after school. Besides, I have some last-minute details to check on."

Delaney hated when Kylie got all mysterious on her. Didn't she know she hated surprises unless she got to spring them? She wanted to daydream about cupcakes, but the script for *Charlotte's Web* was staring at her from the coffee table. After Delaney's initial protest, Ms. Kutchen had convinced her to take on the part of Wilbur the Pig. "If you're going to be a performer one day, you have to understand that you won't always get the part you want," her teacher had explained.

It sounded a lot like "You get what you get, and you don't get upset" to Delaney. But she did love singing—and it was one of the leads. So she agreed.

"How's the musical coming?" her mom asked, flopping down next to her on the couch. She kicked off her shoes and put her feet up.

"Okay, I guess." Delaney shrugged.

Her mom picked up the script and flipped through it. "I love this story. It always makes me cry." She rubbed her belly and smiled. "My favorite part is when Charlotte's three baby daughters hatch and stay behind with Wilbur."

Ugh, Delaney thought. More baby talk! "You're forgetting that all the rest of the spiders fly away and desert him."

Her mother rumpled Delaney's bangs. "You haven't deserted me yet," she said, planting a kiss on her daughter's forehead. "You're always my best girl."

"What if you have another girl? Will I still be your best girl then?" Delaney asked.

"Laney, honey, you'll always be my baby—and my first one. That's a very special place in my heart that no one else can hold."

"Or what if it's a boy? You'll have to go cheer him on at soccer practice, and you won't be able to come see me in my shows!"

Mrs. Noonan chuckled. "I don't think the baby—either he or she—will be playing soccer for a few years. I'll be there—front row, center. I promise. I love watching you shine onstage, honey. And I love you."

Delaney knew it was true. Her mom loved her. But she wasn't sure how things would change when there was another Noonan kid to love. It made her sad just to think about it. Maybe it was selfish, but she wanted her mom all to herself! She loved how they went to see Broadway shows together and snuggled on the couch watching *America's Got Talent.* A new baby would be a lot of work—exhausting work, if Milly was any indication! What if her mom didn't have time or energy for her anymore? What if she became just an afterthought?

☆ ☮ ☆

The thought of the new baby kept nagging away at her even the next day, as Kylie called the cupcake club meeting to order. Peace, Love, and Cupcakes met once a week in the Blakely Elementary School teachers' lounge. It was a time to go through all their cupcake business: what orders were in the lineup for this week; what recipes needed to be created and tested; and of course, who would be doing what.

While it was a big baking business, it was also a lot of fun and a great way for the girls to bond. Juliette, Kylie's drama teacher, was the one who had suggested they start the club. Kylie had found each of the original fab foursome, and they had learned not just how to bake and frost delicious cupcakes, but what it meant to be true friends. With the addition of Delaney, the club clicked even more. No matter what sweet surprise came their way, the girls knew they could handle it together.

Delaney wanted to be excited about this VIP order, but every time she closed her eyes, all she could see was her mom cuddling a tiny bundle in her arms—and her standing on the sidelines.

"So as I told you all, this is a VIP order—and it's very hush-hush," Kylie began.

"Why all the secrecy?" Lexi asked. "Are we baking cupcakes for the White House or something?"

Juliette, the club's advisor, shook her head. "Nope. Think closer to home."

"The Knicks? The Giants? OMG, are we making cupcakes for the Mets?" Sadie piped up.

"Uh-uh," Kylie replied. "No sports teams. I'll give you one more hint. Delaney will be very excited about this order."

"You already said it's not a pop star's b-day or a red-carpet premiere," Delaney said. "Beyond that, what would make me excited?"

"How about knowing if you're having a baby brother or sister?" Kylie beamed.

Delaney wanted to scream. This was the big surprise? This was the VIP? The *baby*?

"Your friend Sophie's mom called. She wants to throw a

baby shower on the seventeenth," Kylie explained. "I spoke to your mom, and she wants us to make twelve dozen gender-reveal cupcakes. You bite into them, and it's either pink cream for a girl or blue for a boy."

"That is so cool!" Lexi cried. "I want to do little baby rattles in fondant on top—or little duckies, or pacifiers!"

"The coolest thing is that no one will know the baby's gender until the party," Kylie added.

"Well, someone will have to know," Sadie pointed out. "The person who puts in the pink or blue filling."

Juliette nodded. "Mrs. Noonan's doctor is going to give her an envelope Friday with the sonogram results and she's going to give it to me and I'll fill the cupcakes. Not even your mom and dad or any of you girls will know 'til the party. It'll be a fantastic surprise. Doesn't that sound great, Delaney?"

Delaney tried to feel excited. She tried to feel anything. But the most she could manage was numb. It was all happening so quickly, and now even her cupcake club had "gone baby" on her! Her parents had bought a stroller, a baby swing, a bouncy seat, a crib, a changing table, and boxes of diapers stacked to the ceiling. Her mom wanted her help in choosing a mobile. ("The zoo animals or the moon and stars? Should it play 'Twinkle, Twinkle, Little Star' or 'Rock-a-Bye Baby'?"). Her dad was even reading *What to Expect When You're Expecting*. It was ridiculous! There were so many details and plans, all for this tiny person who didn't even exist yet!

"Delaney?" Kylie nudged her. "Aren't you excited?"

"I guess," she answered quietly.

"Talk to me about flavors," Jenna said, grabbing a piece of paper and a pencil. "I need to get shopping for ingredients."

"Delaney, what do you think your mom would like?" Juliette asked her.

She wracked her brain, trying to envision what kind of cupcake her mom would want. She wasn't much of a chocolate person, and vanilla was so…well, vanilla. Anything Berry wouldn't be "berry" special. Then it came to her…

"Laffy Taffy."

"What?" Jenna asked. "As in the candy?"

"It's our favorite whenever we go to the movies together. My mom and I shared a big pack of Laffy Taffy when we went to see *Les Mis* on the big screen. It always makes her smile."

"So much for being serious…" Jenna muttered. "But it's doable. We could melt the taffy and fold it into the frosting. Maybe color it sunshiny yellow—which works for a boy or a girl."

"And let's do a lemonade cupcake," Kylie suggested. "Something to balance out the sweetness of the frosting."

Jenna smacked her lips together. "Yup, I can taste that working well together. Lemonade Laffy Taffy Cupcakes it is!"

7

Down on the Farm

At the *Charlotte's Web* rehearsal the next day, Delaney tried to focus on her lines and ignore the fact that a pink, wiggly tail was pinned to the butt of her jeggings.

"You look cute, Laney," Sophie giggled. "The snout… it's really you."

"Yeah, yeah," Delaney replied. "At least I don't have legs hanging all over me." Attached to Sophie's black sweatshirt were four long, black spider legs. She used one to swat Delaney over the head. "Come on, have some fun!"

Since the babysitting episode with Milly, Delaney had learned that she could be herself *and* be responsible. So even in a pig costume, she would give the part her serious attention. She just wished everything and everyone in her life wasn't baby-crazy!

"This big barnyard scene should be a showstopper," Ms. Kutchen directed them. "Cows and lambs, you're in the back. Wilbur, Templeton the Rat, and the geese, you're up front. Charlotte, climb up on the step stool above them."

The kids all stood there, looking bored. "This is so lame," Harrison grumped. He wasn't thrilled to be playing a dirty rat and yanked at his long, black tail. "Can't I be a rat without a tail? Maybe a leather jacket and sunglasses?"

"Like a biker rat?" Delaney teased. "Maybe you can ride around the barnyard on a moped."

"Exactly!" Harrison replied. "That's what I'm talking about!"

Ms. Kutchen handed out sheet music. "Really?" Harrison groaned. "'Homer Zuckerman had a farm, E I E I O'?"

Sophie shook her head. "We have to do something, Laney. Musicals are not Ms. Kutchen's thing. *Charlotte's Web* is going to be the laughingstock of the Weber Day School mini-term."

"You're not kidding," Olivia Issacman, aka Gussy the Goose, whispered. "All I do is sit here laying eggs! I don't even quack."

"Geese don't quack," Harrison corrected her. "They honk."

"That's even worse!" Olivia groaned.

The old Delaney would have jumped in and rallied the troops. She would have broken into a crazy rendition of "Who Let the Pigs Out?" and led a conga line across the stage. But the new Delaney had to be both clever and practical—she'd learn that from her babysitting escapade. She had a role to play and directions to follow. Still, there might be a way to make Ms. Kutchen's musical just a little cooler and more, well, fun. She raised her hand.

"Ms. Kutchen, do I stand in front of the cows during the E I E I O part, or behind them?"

Sophie rolled her eyes. "Laney, snap out of it! Please!"

Delaney hushed her. "Relax, Soph. I have a plan."

"Um, let's try it in front," Ms. Kutchen replied, checking the notes on her clipboard. She got out her harmonica and blew a note. "Everybody, on the count of three, let's try 'Homer Zuckerman Had a Farm'…"

Delaney's hand shot up again. "Yes, Delaney?" Ms. Kutchen sighed.

"I think maybe everyone knows this song—there's no element of surprise," she said.

Ms. Kutchen raised an eyebrow. "What do you mean? It's a classic."

"I just mean that *Charlotte's Web* has a message that's just as important today as it was when it was published in 1952. Shouldn't we somehow communicate that?"

Delaney knew that Ms. Kutchen loved when kids participated in class discussions and had strong opinions about the books the class was reading.

"And what do you think that message is, Delaney?" Her teacher took the bait.

Delaney thought hard for a moment. She twirled a strand of strawberry blond hair around her fingertips. "Well, it's about friendship. How important it is to stand by the people who are important to you. To be there when they need you. And it's about the cycle of life. When Charlotte dies, her babies are born."

"And even though we're all animals, we act like people," Sophie added. "Charlotte is an insect, but she has human thoughts and feelings. She really cares about Wilbur and wants to save his life."

"And Templeton figures out he can eat the pig's slop— which is really pretty disgusting, but I guess, smart," Harrison threw in.

"He means that he's a survivor," Delaney explained. "He may seem mean and selfish, but he actually does help Charlotte and Wilbur. He's not as tough as he wants everyone to believe." She glared at Harrison.

"Yeah, that's what I said…" he added.

Ms. Kutchen nodded her head. "I'm very impressed. Maybe I should let you guys direct the musical."

"Yes!" Delaney pumped her fist in the air. "I mean, yeah, that would be really great if we could pitch in."

Ms. Kutchen handed Delaney her clipboard. "Okay, Delaney. This barnyard scene is all yours. What do you think we should do to make it better?"

Sophie gave Delaney a little push forward. "Go on! Work your magic."

Delaney walked around the stage, taking it all in. How could she turn the Old McDonald song into anything remotely cool?

"I think we should rap it. You know, make it really modern and edgy."

"Totally!" Sophie backed her up. "Like Justin Timberlake…or Macklemore."

Delaney tapped her sneaker on the stage to start the rhythm. "Homer Zuckerman had a farm. *Give it up! Give it up!* Had a farm. There were sheep and cows, and they rapped along. *Give it up! Give it up!* On the farm!"

"A rat called Templeton had lots of charm. *Give it up! Give it up!* On the farm!" Harrison added.

"And a goose named Gussy became a mom. *Give it up! Give it up!* On the farm!" Olivia chimed in.

"Then there was Wilbur—who felt alarm. *Give it up! Give it up!* On the farm!" Delaney rapped. "His best friend, Charlotte, said, 'Fear no harm!' *Give it up! Give it up!* On the farm!"

"And that little black spider spun a yarn. *Give it up! Give it up!* On the farm!" Sophie added.

"Hold on! Hold on!" Ms. Kutchen stopped them.

Uh-oh, Delaney thought. She hates this idea.

"I think this is amazing! I want to write it all down and figure out how you can bust some moves in the barnyard. Delaney, I'm counting on you for the choreography as well."

"Hooray!" the class cheered.

"You did it, Delaney," Sophie whispered. "You saved our musical. *Charlotte's Web* is going to rock, and we owe it all to you."

8

Up, Up, and Away

The more the class rehearsed, the more Delaney began to get excited about the musical. She even recruited Lexi with her strong artistic sense to help them design a cool backdrop for the stage.

"I think it should be a giant spider's web," Delaney told her friend as she sketched an arch and crisscrossed black lines over it.

"Uh-huh." Lexi nibbled on her pencil eraser. "I see what you mean. That would give the words in the web a lot of visual impact. The design could be very minimalist...almost like the original pen lines of the Garth Williams illustrations."

"In English, Lex," Delaney replied. "Not Artist."

"I think the whole stage should like the inside of a book: white background with black lines and type. And we could use silver lanyard to weave the web."

"Like the stuff I make key chains out of at Camp Chicopee?" Delaney asked. "I'm really good at a box stitch."

"Exactly! It's strong and it's shiny. It would be perfect."

Lexi drew a web with the words "Some Pig" in the middle.

"You know what would even be cooler?" Delaney asked. "If we could somehow hang Sophie from the top of the stage and have her swing around the web."

Lexi gulped. "You want to fly your friend through the air? That sounds scary to me."

"What if we tied a rope around her waist or something?" Delaney suggested. "I saw *Peter Pan* on Broadway last year, and the actors who played Peter, Wendy, Michael, and John flew all over the place. And what about Elphaba? She flies on her broomstick and defies gravity in *Wicked*."

Lexi shook her head. "Those are professional productions. There are probably a million pulleys and wires that they use to do it."

"We don't need a million…just maybe one or two," Delaney insisted. "You can't really be a spider unless you spin a web, right?"

☆✌☆

Delaney made a few phone calls and asked for a few favors before explaining her idea to Sophie. "Let me get this straight," her friend said. "You want to put a harness around my waist and swing me around in the air?"

"Pretty much." Delaney smiled. "What do you think?"

"I think you're nuts," Sophie exclaimed. "I'm afraid of heights, Laney! There is no way I am going up in the air."

"It'll be perfectly safe!" Delaney insisted. "We'll try it out first before we even show it to Ms. Kutchen. Please, Soph? Don't you want this to be the best mini-term musical ever?"

Sophie pouted. "Of course I do. I just want to live to tell about it."

Delaney placed an arm around her friend's shoulder. "Trust me. I've got it all worked out. I even asked my friend Sadie to bring her two brothers and meet us here. They're really strong, and they can hoist you to the ceiling, no prob. And her dad is a contractor and sent over everything we need."

"The ceiling? How high is the ceiling?" Sophie gulped. "I really don't know about this, Laney…"

Delaney had to think of something, anything, that would convince her friend to take the leap. "We're going to dim all the lights and shine a spotlight right on you. It's going to be like a Cirque du Soleil act. Everyone oohing and ahhing…"

Sophie bit her lip. "You think so?" If there was one thing she couldn't resist, it was a moment in the spotlight.

Delaney nodded. "Totally. I wouldn't be surprised if you got a standing ovation."

"Okay…" Sophie hesitated. "I guess I could try it. Once."

"Great! Be in the auditorium during last period. Sadie, Tyler, and Corey will meet us there. And maybe you should bring a helmet…"

"A helmet!" Sophie gasped. "Why do I need a helmet?"

"Better safe than sorry, my mom always says." Delaney smiled. "See ya in a few!"

☆ ☮ ☆

When Sophie arrived in the auditorium, Sadie's brothers had already set up a makeshift pulley system by looping a long cable through the truss hanging over the stage. One end of the cable was attached to a harness, and the other to a belt around Tyler's waist.

"Thanks for doing this, guys," Delaney said, examining the pulley. "I owe you."

"You sure do," Corey said. "I believe the price we agreed on was two dozen of my favorite brownie fudge cupcakes with peanut butter frosting."

"And two dozen red velvets for me—with those itty-bitty chocolate chips inside," Tyler added.

"Done." Delaney nodded. "You drive a hard bargain. Now fill me in on how this all works."

"It's pretty simple," Tyler explained. "I once made a tire swing for the tree house in my backyard the same way. I'm the anchor. You're the swing."

"I hate swings," Sophie muttered, staring up at the ceiling. "That looks really, really high."

"I'd say it's about twenty feet," Corey said, munching on a bag of potato chips. "Give or take a foot or two."

Sophie grabbed Delaney's arm. "I am not going up there. It's way too high!"

Delaney held out the harness and began to wrap it around Sophie's waist. "It's really easy, I promise. Have you ever done one of those fun bungee trampolines at the Firemen's Carnival? The one where they pull you up, and you bounce and do backflips?"

Sophie nodded. "Oh, yeah. I did it once."

"See! And it was no biggie, right?"

"I threw up," Sophie said. "Like ten times."

"I wish you had told us to bring an umbrella," Tyler said, making a face.

"You're gonna be fine," Delaney said, crossing her fingers. "Let's take it slow and see how it goes." She secured the helmet on Sophie's head and took a step back.

Corey stood in front of Tyler and began to pull the rope. Sophie jolted into the air.

"*Eeek!*" she screamed. "This is scary! Put me down!"

"You're only about six inches off the ground," Corey said, chuckling. "What a wimp!"

"Point your toes and wave your arms in the air like a spider," Delaney coached her. "Like this."

"Easy for you to say," Sophie shot back. "Your feet are on the ground."

"Going up!" Corey called, and Sophie climbed a few feet above the stage.

Sophie squeezed her eyes tightly shut. "I can't look!" Corey tugged once again, and she rose even higher.

"Try and swing. Use your legs and arms, and we'll pull you left and right," Delaney directed her. "Cue the lights!"

"Aye, aye, captain!" Sadie shouted from the lighting

panel in the back of the theater. With the flip of a switch, the entire auditorium went dark. Sophie screamed.

"I'm scared of the dark!"

"I thought you said she was scared of heights," Tyler said to Delaney.

"I'm scared of both!" Sophie yelled.

"Where's the spotlight?" Delaney shouted to Sadie.

"Working on it! There are so many buttons on this thing…"

Suddenly, a bright, white light hit Sophie midair.

"Awesome!" Delaney called to her. "You're a star!"

Sophie opened her eyes and looked down. Everything and everyone looked so small and far away. "OMG. I'm going to be sick."

"No! No!" Tyler ducked behind Corey for cover. "No puking, please!"

"You're doing great, Soph," Delaney said. "Wanna try a few spidery moves?"

Corey pulled the rope sharply to the right, and Sophie soared across the stage.

"Not so fast!" she screamed. "I'm getting dizzy!"

He tugged in the opposite direction, and she flew back the other way.

"She's a spider…not a jet plane!" Delaney scolded him. "Slow and steady."

"Yeah, slow and steady," Sophie repeated. "What she said!"

Sophie began to swing back and forth like a pendulum. She stretched out her legs and arms. "You look great!" Delaney said. "How do you feel?"

"Okay, I guess," she replied. "I think I'm getting used to it."

"See? I told you there was nothing to it." Delaney smiled.

The rope suddenly slipped, and Sophie lurched in the air. "*EEEEEEE!*" she screamed. "I'm falling!"

"Relax," Corey said. "My hand slipped. Potato-chip grease."

"Amateurs!" Delaney barked. "Take her up again. Let's try and make the swinging more rhythmic and graceful."

Just then the spotlight cut off and they were once again in the pitch-dark.

"I hate the dark!" Sophie screamed. "Remember?"

"I know, I know!" Sadie was hitting buttons frantically on the panel. "I think we blew a fuse."

Suddenly, there was a loud *thump*.

"What was that?" Delaney gulped. "Soph, you okay?"

"Fine!" Sophie called back. "I landed on something soft." The lights came up.

"That would be me!" Tyler said. He was lying face-down on the stage, and Sophie was standing on top of him. "Get off!"

Tyler rose to his feet and punched his younger brother in the arm. "You just had to eat those chips, didn't you?"

Corey waved his fingers in the air. "Oops. I guess I slipped again."

Delaney helped Sophie out of her helmet and harness. "The important thing is that we learned this will work—if Corey skips the greasy snack food." She shot him a look, then turned back to Sophie.

"What do you think? Can Charlotte do some spinning in the musical?"

Sophie rested her hands on her hips. "You know, I think I might just have a future in Cirque du Soleil."

Delaney hugged her. "You were air-mazing," she teased. "Gussy the Goose couldn't have flown any better."

"Chip?" Corey offered them the bag. "All this flying made me hungry."

9

Bibbidi Bobbidi Birthday

Delaney had never summoned the girls together for a cupcake club meeting—but this was a cupcake 911. When they all gathered in her living room, she stood on the coffee table and clapped her hands so they'd all stop talking and pay close attention.

"PLCers, listen up," she began. "We have a cupcake crisis that needs our help." She was actually getting a lot better at this "serious" stuff!

"We're all ears," Kylie said. "What's up, Laney?"

"Ms. Roveen called, and the baker who was doing Milly's birthday cake broke her arm," she explained. "Her party is this weekend!"

"Wait, who's Milly?" Jenna asked. "And what kind of party?"

"A two-year-old Cinderella birthday party," Delaney replied. "With about two dozen little kids coming!"

"No sweat," Sadie said. "We've done tons of kid birthday parties. We can do some of those confetti cupcakes with rainbow sprinkles..."

Lexi grabbed her sketchbook. "How 'bout the usual: little fondant balloons on top?"

"No! No! No!" Delaney protested. "This isn't just any kid's birthday. It's Milly! I want it to be really special for her."

Kylie nodded. She knew Delaney's first babysitting job had meant a lot to her. Obviously, the little girl did too. "What were you thinking, Laney? Little glass slippers on top of the cupcakes?"

"Bigger," Delaney commanded. "Think bigger."

"Well, we could do a coach made out of mini cupcakes," Lexi thought out loud. "Like a centerpiece for the table."

Delaney shook her head. "Bigger."

"Ooh! How about Cinderella's castle made out of cupcakes?" Jenna suggested. "A three-foot-tall castle made of cupcakes would be *muy bonita*—very pretty!"

"Even bigger," Delaney insisted. "I want Princess Milly's cupcakes to be magical. Like the Fairy Godmother in Cinderella."

Her eyes lit up. "That's it! That's what we should

do! We should make the Fairy Godmother's skirt out of cupcakes—and she should come to the party and cast a magic spell!"

Lexi raised an eyebrow. "A skirt made out of cupcakes? Can we do that? I mean, this isn't an episode of *Project Runway!*"

"I think the cupcakes would fall off the fabric." Sadie pondered. "How would we pin them on? Cupcakes are heavy!"

"I'm not sure. We'd have to try it out," Delaney said. "Please, let's try!"

"All in favor of Delaney's project-cupcake skirt say 'sprinkles!'" Kylie said.

"Sprinkles!" Sadie, Delaney, Lexi, and Kylie all shouted.

Jenna frowned. "Okay, you've got my vote—but I'm just not sure about this. Besides the obvious fashion emergency, where are we gonna find a Fairy Godmother on this short notice?"

All eyes turned to Delaney. "You *are* a really good singer…" Lexi said. "I could see you Bibbidi-Bobbidi-Booing…"

Delaney pictured herself waltzing around Milly's party, waving a magic wand, as the toddlers squealed with delight. "I'll do it. On one condition."

"Oh, boy…here it comes!" Sadie chuckled.

"I want the cupcakes to be Milly's favorite flavors."

"I knew we were in trouble," Jenna groaned. "Okay, let's have it. What are Milly's fave flavors?"

Delaney jumped off the table, grabbed a spoon, and waved it in the air like a wand. "Cheerios and applesauce!"

☆ ☮ ☆

The next day, the cupcake club gathered in the teachers' lounge at Blakely Elementary to make some magic in the kitchen.

"Okay, I found a few cupcakes that use applesauce," Kylie said, pulling out her binder of recipes. "It actually makes the cake very moist."

The first version called for real chunks of apple in the center of the cupcake. "What is this?" Jenna asked, picking a seed out of her teeth. She looked at Sadie who was coring the apples and slicing them. "You can't have any seeds in the batter."

Sadie sighed. "I'm sorry. They just keep sneaking in there…"

Kylie pulled a seed out of Sadie's hair. "They keep sneaking in here too!"

The next recipe called for caramel to ooze out of the center of the apple cupcake.

Jenna took a bite and licked her lips. "It's a little sticky," she said.

"Define *sticky*," Lexi said. "Is that a good thing or a bad thing?"

"I'll let you know when I can open my mouth. My gums are glued together."

Kylie took out the very last recipe she had found. This one was an apple spice cupcake with a hint of nutmeg and cinnamon.

"Easy on the spices," Jenna warned them as they measured a teaspoon into the batter. "Just a hint—not a handful."

They popped the batter in the muffin tin and watched the cupcakes rise and turn golden brown in the oven.

"Looks good," Jenna said, sniffing the finished product. Lexi had piped on a dollop of vanilla buttercream frosting. She broke the cupcake open with a fork and sampled the cake. Then the frosting. Then the cake and the frosting together.

"Well?" Delaney asked anxiously. "Is it a winner?"

Jenna gave them the thumbs-up. "This one has a really nice, spicy apple flavor," she said. "Like warm apple pie. And the sweet frosting is a nice balance."

Lexi passed out her sketches. "I think we should color

the frosting purple—just like the Fairy Godmother's cape and skirt. I could maybe use some luster dust to give them a magical sparkle."

"Let's not forget the Cheerios!" Delaney reminded them. She popped one in her mouth and stuck out her tongue.

"Oh, right." Jenna rolled her eyes. "How could we forget?"

"I gave that a lot of thought," Lexi said, smiling, "and I think I have a great solution." She pulled a plastic bag out of her backpack. Inside were a "necklace" and "bracelet" made out of Cheerios and mini-marshmallows. "I think we could do Cheerios jewelry for all the little princesses at the party. Whaddaya think, Delaney?"

Delaney slipped the necklace over her head and bit off a crunchy O. "I think Milly will love it."

"So all that leaves us is making the cupcake costume," Kylie said, checking items off her list. "Sadie, do you think your dad can build us something?"

"My dad is a contractor—not a fashion designer," Sadie said, considering the idea.

"My mom can help with the design and sewing," Jenna offered. "She's an amazing seamstress. She can make a beautiful cape and hood. But your dad will have to find a way to make the cupcakes stick to the skirt. And the skirt to stick to Delaney."

Delaney looked at the sketch Lexi had made on her pad. It showed a giant dome made out of cupcakes and a little head and arms perched on top. "Is that supposed to be me?" she asked. "How am I supposed to get into that thing? And how do I move around?"

"I hadn't really thought about that," Lexi admitted. "Maybe you can climb up a ladder in the back? And we can carry you inside?"

"Forklift?" Jenna teased. "We could just hoist you off the back of Sadie's dad's pickup truck."

☆ ⊕ ☆

It was clear that the cupcake club needed some expert advice. So the next evening, the girls all gathered in Mr. Harris's home workshop.

"My dad has some great ideas," Sadie said proudly. "Tell them!"

"I think we can do a frame for the skirt out of chicken wire and spray foam filler," he explained. "How many cupcakes were you thinking?"

"Three hundred...give or take a few," Lexi replied. "That should cover all sides of the skirt."

Delaney's eyes grew wide. "Three hundred cupcakes? That's gonna weigh a ton!"

"Which is why your skirt will have wheels," Mr. Harris continued. "So you can roll around the room."

"Did I happen to mention I am a total klutz on roller skates, skateboards, bikes, or anything involving wheels?" Delaney sighed.

"It's true," Kylie agreed. "We made go-carts at Camp Chicopee, and Delaney crashed hers right into the lake."

"It'll look like you're magically gliding around the room," Sadie assured Delaney. "Maybe we can even add some lights."

Mr. Harris examined his blueprint. "I think I could run some fiber-optic cable through the skirt frame—give it a little twinkle."

Delaney wasn't quite sure—but there was no time to waste. They had three days to bake, decorate, sew, and construct the entire costume. Kylie read her mind.

"It'll be awesome, Laney," she said, giving her friend a hug. "You just practice your song and your wand waving, and leave everything else to us."

Without a real Fairy Godmother to make it come together, Delaney wasn't sure the costume would be ready in time for Milly's birthday. But she crossed her fingers... and hoped for the best!

10

A Royal Celebration

Delaney looked in the mirror and admired her reflection. The purple hooded cape Jenna's mom had made her was amazing! It was tied with a huge pink bow and beaded with clear sequins so that it shimmered as she waved her arms in the air. She'd even sprinkled flour in her hair to look like a real fairy godmother—white hair and all!

"Can I sneak a peek pre-performance?" her mom said, poking her head into the bedroom.

"Whaddaya think?" Delaney asked. "Does it scream 'Fairy Godmother'?"

Mrs. Noonan motioned for her to do a twirl. "I think it's gorgeous. But aren't you missing something?" She pointed to Delaney's legs, which were bare—except for a pair of frayed denim shorts and high-top purple sneakers. "I've never seen a Fairy Godmother in shorts and Nikes."

"I haven't seen the skirt yet," Delaney said. "I'm kind of scared to."

Her mom planted a kiss on her forehead. "I'm sure it'll be great—and you'll be a fabulous Fairy Godmother. Milly will love it."

Her tummy gave a kick. "Ooh! Did you feel that? The baby likes your look!"

Delaney rolled her eyes. "The baby can't see through your belly," she said. "But thanks Baby Noonan for the thumbs-up."

Her mom sat down on Delaney's bed. It was getting harder and harder for her to stand for too long. The baby was growing like crazy! "So, are you feeling a little better about the whole baby situation?" she asked Delaney. "I want you to be happy, honey."

"I am," Delaney said. "I guess at first I was just scared and kind of in shock. I really didn't know what kind of a big sister I'd be."

Her mom placed Delaney's hand on her belly. "And you know now?" she asked.

"I think I can handle it," Delaney replied. "Thanks to Silly Milly and all the PLC girls showing me how."

Her mom nodded. "I always knew you could. And I

know you're going to be such a great help to me when the baby comes."

Delaney smiled. "Do you kind of wish you didn't have to wait two more months to meet Baby Noonan?"

Her mom picked up the purple glittery wand that was resting on Delaney's bed. "It would be so much easier if a fairy godmother could just wave this and I could skip the entire labor and delivery!"

Delaney could tell that her mom was nervous. "It'll be okay," she said, hugging her. "You did a pretty good job with me."

Mrs. Noonan playfully tapped Delaney on the head with the wand. "I certainly did. Now you'd better get to Milly's party before I turn you into a pumpkin!"

☆ ☮ ☆

When Mr. Harris pulled up in his truck, Kylie was already in the back and Sadie was seated up front next to her dad. "We're meeting Jenna and Lexi at the party," she explained. "There kind of wasn't enough room for everyone and the skirt."

She motioned to the back of the truck where there appeared to be a huge mountain covered in purple cupcakes. "Whaddaya think of your costume, Laney?" Sadie asked.

Mr. Harris had molded chicken wire into a dome and stuffed it with newspaper and spray foam, then painted it over with lavender paint. The cupcakes were tacked to the hardened foam with toothpicks. Delaney stared. The skirt looked like the piñata she had made for her Spanish class project out of papier-mâché—only about ten times the size. And there was no candy going in it—she was the filling!

"It's *huge*!" she gasped. "Seriously! You guys got carried away!"

"You did say you wanted to give Milly a birthday she'd never forget," Kylie reminded her. "So we went a little over the top."

"Dad did a really great job," Sadie boasted. "You just climb on in there, stand on the platform, give a little kick, and roll around. I tried it out and it works perfectly."

For you, maybe! Delaney thought to herself. Sadie had half-a-dozen skateboarding trophies on her shelf at home!

"Too late to change your mind," Kylie said, poking her. "I think we're here."

The truck pulled up in front of Ms. Roveen's house. A path of balloons lead up to the door, and little Milly—in a pale blue Cinderella gown—was jumping up and down on the front steps.

"Don't let her see me!" Delaney said, ducking down in the backseat. "I want this to be a surprise."

"No prob, Your Godmotherness," Sadie teased. "We'll make sure all the kids are inside before we roll you out."

Sadie and Kylie greeted Ms. Roveen and ushered the birthday girl back into the house.

"Okay, Delaney," Mr. Harris said, rolling the cupcake-covered skirt down a ramp off the back of the truck. "Up ya go!"

He linked his hands together making a step to boost her up. "You'll feel the platform under your feet when you get down inside. There's a hole in the bottom so you can kick-start yourself in any direction you want to go. Like a skateboard—with about three hundred cupcakes on top of it!"

Delaney wiggled into the waist of the skirt. It was both stiff and sticky at the same time.

"Wait! Wait!" Lexi cried. They had just arrived in Jenna's stepdad's car and pulled up behind the truck. "You're mushing my piping!" She and Jenna jumped out and held her under the arms for support. "Easy…easy…"

Delaney felt the wooden platform below her. "Okay, I think I'm in." She tried to inch forward or even roll side to side, but the skirt wouldn't budge.

"It's too heavy with me in it," she sighed. "Now what?"

Mr. Harris got down on the ground and examined the wheels on the platform. "It'll be fine on a smooth surface. Let's just get you off the lawn and into the house."

It took all three of them to lift her gently up the two front steps. "I'll get the front, you get the back," Mr. Harris instructed the girls. "I'll lift from below and you give a push."

It took about a dozen tries—and they lost a few cupcakes—but Delaney was finally at the front door. Lexi did a quick touchup, refastening the cupcakes and piping them with a bag of purple frosting she had tossed in her purse ("just in case!").

"You look like the little plastic figure topper on a huge wedding cake," Kylie said, giggling. Delaney wished she had a mirror to see what she looked like. She felt pretty ridiculous, but hoped she didn't look that way. Mr. Harris flipped a switch on a tiny remote and the skirt lit up with white twinkly lights.

Ms. Roveen opened the door and gasped. "Wow! That is really something!" she whispered. "The kids are going to go nuts!"

"You ready?" Kylie asked Delaney. "It's showtime!"

Delaney stared at the entrance way. "I'm not sure I'm going to fit!"

Mr. Harris whipped out the tape measure in his tool belt to measure the opening and the width of the god-mother skirt. "It'll be close. I think we should take off some cupcakes to make room."

Lexi groaned. "I'll have to pipe them all over again!" But Kylie was already handing her, Ms. Roveen, Jenna, and Sadie handfuls. "Sorry, Delaney—your dress needs to go on a diet…"

With a gentle push, she made it through the door frame with not an inch to spare.

"Okay, hand me the cupcakes and I'll put them back on…again!" Lexi said. She toothpicked and piped 'til the skirt was whole again.

"You're good to go, Laney," Kylie said. Thankfully, the hallway and living room were wide open.

Delaney closed her eyes and tried to get into character. "Okay, hit it!" she announced.

Sadie pushed a button on her MP3 player. Music filled the air, and all the children rushed into the center of the living room to see what was going on. Delaney flung her arms up in the air and pushed off with her toes, willing the skirt to roll forward. Like magic, it did!

"Salagadoola, mechicka boola," she began to belt.

"Oooh!" Milly squealed with delight. "Bibbi Boo!"

Delaney continued rolling down the hallway and into the foyer, waving her arms as she sang. This is pretty easy! she praised herself. Who knew I could rock and roll…literally?

Then, all of a sudden, just before she reached the living room and the cheering kids, she felt the skirt hit a bump. It tilted back—taking her with it.

She looked down and saw the problem: she had completely forgotten about the two steps that led into the sunken living room. As she bumped over the first, then the second, she and the mountain of cupcakes began to topple backward.

"Help! Where are the brakes?" she screamed. "I can't stop!"

"Wait! No!" Kylie ran after her, trying to catch her from falling. She and Jenna held out their arms and braced themselves. As the skirt and Delaney rocked backward, they caught it and pushed hard the other way. They were covered in cupcakes, but at least Delaney was still standing.

"Phew! That was close!" Lexi said, uncovering her eyes. But she spoke too soon. Now, Delaney was tipping forward, about to fall right into the crowd of unsuspecting toddlers.

Delaney tried to lean back, but it was no use. The skirt was too tall, too wide, and too heavy. "Outta the way! Outta the way!" she screamed, but the kids continued watching her in awe. She looked like a human seesaw, and they thought it was part of the show!

"Everybody over here!" Ms. Roveen shouted. She and the other moms managed to herd them all back to a corner of the room before Delaney completely tipped over. She landed facedown with a *splat* on the carpet, in a puddle of cake and purple frosting.

"Oh my gosh, Laney, are you okay?" Kylie kneeled over her.

"I've fallen and I can't get up," Delaney whispered. "This is so embarrassing!" Her face was smooshed into the carpet, and her arms were pinned to her sides.

The girls and Mr. Harris managed to pull her back upright, but most of the cupcakes were totaled. "Oh, no," Lexi said. She was practically in tears. "Our beautiful cupcakes!"

Mr. Harris helped Delaney climb out of the skirt. Her white hair was now covered in purple frosting, and the cape looked crazy with her cutoffs and high-tops.

"Nice outfit," Sadie teased. "What do you call it? Funky Fairy Godmother?"

Delaney couldn't worry about how ridiculous she looked. She had to find Milly! She hoped she wasn't crying or scared by the whole Fairy Godmother fiasco.

She spotted the little girl in her mother's arms—but she wasn't crying. In fact, she was cracking up!

"Dee-lay-nee go *boom*! Dee-lay-nee go *boom*!" she said over and over.

Delaney wiped some frosting off her cheek and dotted it on Milly's nose. "Did you like my silly Fairy Godmother fall?" she asked the little girl. "Was that wobbly or what?"

Milly clapped enthusiastically. None of the other kids looked too disturbed either—they were rolling around in the frosting on the floor, making snow angels in it.

"I never did like that white carpeting," Ms. Roveen said, surveying the chaos. "I guess it'll now be purple polka dot."

"I am so, so sorry!" Delaney said. "I didn't mean to ruin Milly's party—or your rug."

"It's fine. The kids are having a great time," Ms. Roveen replied. "Right, Milly?" Milly was too busy licking the sticky frosting from her fingers to pay any attention.

Lexi appeared with a tray of cupcakes. "I managed to pull some of these off the sides of the skirt and fix the frosting," she said. "Who wants cupcakes?"

"Me!" screamed all the party guests, rushing her.

"I did warn you that I was bad on wheels," Delaney told Kylie.

Kylie shrugged. "Yeah, but you certainly gave Milly a birthday she'll never forget."

Delaney looked over at the birthday girl. She was already on her second cupcake and smiling from ear to ear.

"Oh! I almost forgot!" Delaney said, taking off her Cheerio necklace and looping it around Milly's neck. "Your princess necklace!"

Milly looked at the gift thoughtfully. Then she flung her arms around Delaney's waist. "Love you!" she shouted, before racing back to her friends and the frosting Slip 'n Slide on the carpet.

For a moment, Delaney was speechless. No matter how much she had messed things up, Milly still loved her. Her heart felt so full, she thought it might burst.

"And that is what being a big sister is all about," Ms. Roveen told her. "In your brother's or sister's eyes, you'll always be awesome."

"You're pretty awesome in our eyes too," Kylie said, mopping frosting out of her friend's hair with a pink paper napkin.

Delaney smiled. "Thanks, but next time, let's make sure my cupcake skirt has training wheels."

The Big Reveal

Sophie's mom, Lisa, had pulled out all the stops for the baby shower. "You know my mom," Sophie told Delaney. "She loves to throw a big, over-the-top party."

The entire backyard of the Spivac home was decorated with yellow balloons and streamers. There were five tables and chairs—enough for fifty guests—draped in buttercup yellow linens. And at every place setting was a baby bottle filled with yellow jelly beans.

"What is that?" Delaney asked, pointing to a small kiddie pool inflated in the middle of the main table. Dozens of rubber duckies were floating in it.

"Oh! It's a shower game. You pick up a ducky, and it has a question on the bottom about babies. If you answer it right, you win a prize."

"Great." Delaney rolled her eyes. "Is there a prize for the fewest correct answers? 'Cause that would be me."

"I think you know a lot more than you realize." Sophie gave her friend a hug.

"You've come a long way, Laney. You're going to be a great big sis."

"I second that!" Kylie said, arriving in the garden with the rest of the cupcake club. "Are you excited for the big reveal?"

Truthfully, Delaney had almost forgotten that today was the day she would know if she was getting a little brother or sister. The musical and preparing for Milly's party had kept her so busy that she'd barely had time to worry these days about the baby situation.

"I guess." Delaney tried to sound enthusiastic. She glanced over at her mom and dad who were greeting guests. They looked so happy. Her mom kept rubbing her belly and laughing.

"What do you want more? A brother or a sister?" Lexi asked her.

Delaney considered both possibilities. It would be fun to dress up a little sis and teach her how to be her backup dancer onstage. Then again, maybe a brother would be great for singing duets? He could take the bass, and she could take the melody…

"I dunno. I guess either would be okay."

"Well, it looks like you're going to find out soon. Juliette and Sadie's dad just arrived with the cupcakes," Kylie pointed out.

They rolled in a beautiful white toy box filled with individual cupcake boxes. On the sides of the box, Lexi had painted teddy bears eating cupcakes at a picnic. Delaney's mom gasped when she saw it.

"This is our gift to the baby from the cupcake club," Juliette said, hugging her. "Sadie's dad built it, and Lexi painted it. And we all made the cupcakes for the party."

"I don't know what to say," Delaney's mom replied. There were tears in her eyes. "It's so beautiful. Thank you, girls."

After a lovely luncheon of tea sandwiches, champagne, and lemonade, it was time to hand out the cupcakes.

"Now, no one open your box and take a bite until we give the signal," Juliette explained. The girls circled the room, placing a cupcake box at each plate.

"Pink is a girl, blue is a boy," Kylie added. "And no one knows what's inside except Juliette."

"Not even Delaney," Jenna pointed out. "This is going to be *una enorme sorpresa*—a huge surprise!"

Juliette nodded. "You can say that again. Delaney, do you want to count down for us?"

Delaney stood up at her seat and raised her cupcake box in the air. "On the count of three…one, two, three…*open!*"

All the guests opened their boxes to find a beautiful lemon cupcake with a fondant rubber ducky on top.

"Now everyone, take a bite and shout it out!" Kylie called.

Jenna was the first: "Blue! It's a boy!"

The crowd cheered.

"Wait! I have pink! It's a girl!" Sadie said.

"Me too!" said one partygoer.

"I have blue!" said another.

"Oh my gosh," Kylie said, examining her own pink-filled cupcake. "Juliette must have messed up. She accidentally filled the cupcakes with both colors!"

"It wasn't an accident," Juliette said, beaming. "But I'll let the mother-to-be explain."

All the guests stopped eating and turned to Mrs. Noonan to see what she had to say. "I'm having twins," she said, smiling. "And from the looks of it, it's a boy *and* a girl."

Delaney was too stunned to speak. One baby was nerve-wracking enough…but *two*?

"You okay, Laney?" Sophie asked her. "You look a little pale."

Her mom and dad came over to hug her. "I'm sorry it was a bit of a shocker," Mr. Noonan said. "But your mom and I saw how freaked out you were about the news of one sibling. We thought we'd let it all sink in a little before we told you it was two."

"It's wonderful, isn't it?" her mom asked. "A brother *and* a sister?"

Delaney felt frozen to her seat. She felt like everything around her was happening in slow motion. She could hear her parents and Sophie and Kylie all talking, but none of the words made any sense. She saw the cupcakes…the balloons…the rubber duckies…then everything went black.

The next thing she knew, she was on the floor with a wet burp cloth on her forehead.

"You passed out, honey," her mother said. She looked very worried.

Kylie nodded. "You took a nosedive right into the rubber ducky pool." That explained why her hair was dripping wet!

"It was very dramatic," Sophie said, squeezing her hand. "An award-winning swoon if I ever saw one."

"How many fingers am I holding up?" Kylie asked.

Delaney rubbed her temples. "Two. Really, I'm fine."

"Let's see if your brain is working…" Jenna said. She held up a ducky with a question. "It says, 'What's a binky?'"

Delaney sat up slowly. "A pacifier." Silly Milly had taught her that.

Sadie read another duck: "Name three songs with the word 'baby' in the title."

That was an easy one! "'Baby One More Time' by Britney Spears, 'Always Be My Baby' by Mariah Carey, and 'Don't Worry, Baby' by The Beach Boys," Delaney answered.

Lexi held up a third duck. "Now here's a tough one: 'What are the names of Charlotte's three baby daughters in *Charlotte's Web*?'"

Most of the guests scratched their heads, but Delaney didn't hesitate. She'd read the book more than a dozen times and memorized the script backward and forward. "Joy, Aranea, and Nellie."

"Then this prize must be for you," Mr. Noonan said, handing Delaney a large box wrapped with a yellow bow.

She opened it and gently pulled back the tissue paper. Inside was a T-shirt that read, "I'm the Big Sister."

"You're ready," her mom said, hugging her. "These are

the luckiest little babies in the world to have you for their big sister."

Delaney could feel tears welling up in the corners of her eyes. She *would* make a great big sister. She knew that now—maybe she'd known it all along.

"Step back, give the girl some room to breathe," Jenna said, helping Delaney to her feet.

"Do you want some water?" Mrs. Spivac asked, offering her a glass.

"Nope." Delaney smiled. "But I could really use a cupcake!"

Sweet Serenade

Everything in Delaney's life seemed to be flying by. Before she knew it, the day of the musical was only a week away—and they were still painting sets, sewing costumes, and composing the music.

"Our finale stinks," she told Sophie. "It's the world's most boring death scene. We're seriously going to put the audience to sleep!"

Ms. Kutchen suggested that Charlotte simply fall down dead onstage.

"I could do it like this…" Sophie demonstrated. She spun around in a circle, toppled backward, then landed on the floor with her legs twitching in the air. She made a strange gurgling sound with her throat. "Then fade to black…how's that?"

"Sad…and I don't mean in a makes-me-want-to-cry way," Delaney replied. "I mean we can do better."

Sophie sat up. "Maybe I could fall headfirst in a kiddie pool of rubber duckies," she teased. "That certainly got everyone's attention at the baby shower."

Delaney ignored her. She was thinking. "No, it needs to be more dramatic yet touching—a parting of best friends. Like Elphaba and Glinda in *Wicked* when they sing 'For Good.'"

"You mean we should sing a duet?" Sophie asked. "Okay, I'm in. But what do we sing?"

Delaney considered all the Broadway show tunes she knew, but none of them seemed right. It wasn't often that you found a musical about a pig and a spider.

"I think we're going to have to write our own song," she said finally. She got out a piece of paper and a pencil, and scratched a title on top of the page. It read: "Saying Good-bye."

She began to sing softly. "You and me, me and you. An unusual pair—that's us two."

"Who would have thought that we could be a dynamic duo for eternity?" Sophie continued.

"Perfect!" Delaney said. "Then I could sing, 'This is a journey that will never end. I'm so proud to call you friend.'"

"Oh my gosh, that is *so* beautiful!" Sophie gushed. "I

have goose bumps. Laney, you're a better songwriter than Taylor Swift!"

Delaney paused for a moment, then wrote the next verse: "Everything around us must flow and ebb. Life is fragile, like a spider's web."

Sophie nodded—then made up the final line: "But when you hold someone in your heart, time and death can't tear you apart." She sniffled and wiped her eyes on the back of her sleeve.

Delaney smiled. It was a beautiful song if she did say so herself. It was just the right amount of sentimental mush (as her mom liked to call it) mixed with a catchy tune. She was sure everyone would be humming it when they left the auditorium. "If that doesn't make the audience cry like babies, I don't know what will."

"And speaking of babies…" Sophie poked her. "How's your mom doing?" It had been several weeks since the baby shower, and Delaney had been strangely quiet about the twin situation. Frankly, all her friends had been scared to bring it up!

"She's big. Like *really* big," Delaney said. "She says she feels like a balloon in the Macy's Thanksgiving Day Parade."

"Are you guys all ready? I mean, two babies is a lot to handle."

Delaney was well aware of that! Thanks to all the gifts from friends and family, the nursery was stocked with two of everything: two cribs, two changing tables, two closets filled with blue and pink clothes. They barely had any room in the house for anything non-baby-related. "I guess. We just need names for them. I suggested Gaga and Bieber, but my parents vetoed them."

Sophie giggled. "Really? I can't imagine why! At least you have six more weeks 'til your mom's due date."

Six weeks? Was that all? Sophie couldn't be right…that was right around the corner! She checked her school planner, and sure enough, there was her mom's due date just a few pages away.

"I guess I kinda put it out of my mind." Delaney sighed.

Sophie nodded. "My mom calls that burying your head in the sand. It's when you don't really want to deal with a problem so you just ignore it. When I had no idea what to write my history term paper about and didn't talk to Ms. Mancini, I was doing the same thing."

"Babies are not term papers," Delaney insisted. "But I get what you're saying. After the baby shower,

I promised myself I wasn't going to worry about being a big sister anymore. And now they're going to be here in a few weeks, and I haven't even made the video yet!"

Sophie looked confused. "Video? What video?"

"I was thinking I should make a video for the twins. You know, kind of showing them around," Delaney said. "Like, 'Hey, guys…welcome to my world!'"

"I think it's a great idea—and I can ask my dad if we can borrow his video camera. It's pretty cool. Just promise me you won't watch the last thing he recorded on it."

"What's that?" Delaney asked.

"Getting my braces on—even the green rubber bands. So embarrassing!"

☆ ☮ ☆

Delaney thought her introduction for the twins should be as realistic as possible, so she got her teachers' permission to film in some of her classes. "This is me in P.E.!" Delaney said into the lens. A volleyball went soaring through the air and bounced off her head.

"Noonan! Heads up! Are you in outer space?" Coach Freeman called.

"As you can see, it's not my best subject!" Delaney said before signing off.

In science, she filmed her group's experiment. "The reaction between baking soda and vinegar generates carbon dioxide gas…" she narrated. The beaker Harrison was holding suddenly bubbled up and poured all over the table and the floor.

"Guys! What are you doing—besides making a mess?" Ms. McKneely asked.

"Yeah, not my best subject either," Delaney whispered into the camera.

What she was most excited to film was the cupcake club meeting and all her friends' and Juliette's messages to the babies-to-be.

"Okay, when I say, 'Roll 'em,' start talking," she instructed her advisor.

"*Bonjour, bebes!*" Juliette said in her native French-Canadian. "*Bienvenue au monde!* Welcome to the world!"

Kylie was next. "What am I supposed to say?"

"Say something you think they should know. Something important," Delaney suggested.

Kylie cleared her throat. "Hi, this is Kylie Carson. In case you didn't know, cupcakes are the best thing to eat in the whole world. Better than pizza, better than ice cream, better than anything you can imagine. But I guess you'll be eating baby food for a while, which is pretty gross. Mushed peas and stuff…"

Delaney paused the recording. "Um, I don't have that much memory left, Kyles. You wanna speed it up?"

Kylie continued: "Anywho…we have this awesome cupcake club called Peace, Love, and Cupcakes. Delaney is not just a part of it—she's a *special* part of it. She gives our club its sparkle. When you meet her, you'll understand why. Anytime you're feeling sad or bored or worried, you have an amazing big sister who knows exactly what to do and say to lift your spirits. Laney is like a sister to all of us, so I know how really lucky you guys are. Oh, and if you ever need to know the lyrics to a song, you don't have to google it. Laney is like an encyclopedia of music."

"Do you think they'll know what Google is?" Lexi asked. "Babies don't google."

"They goo-goo, though," Jenna joked. "Get it?"

Delaney turned the camera to face her. "These are the rest of my friends and fellow cupcake clubbers. They're all pretty crazy—but don't let 'em scare you."

"Hey, I am not loco," Jenna insisted. "Turn that camera my way!

She stood up, took a deep breath, and began to speak. "*Hola, bambinos!* I'm Jenna Medina, and I have twin brothers so I know what you guys are thinking. You're thinking, Gee, we can make twice as much mischief as one little kid! But seriously, two is even better than one. You guys are going to have a really special bond. *Mis hermanos* Manny and Ricky are not just brothers, they're best friends."

"Can I say something?" Lexi piped up. "The world is pretty awesome—and colorful. I can't wait 'til you guys see your first sunrise…or fireworks exploding on the Fourth of July! I can even help you finger paint when you're ready. I love to finger paint…"

"Me next!" Sadie said, jumping in front of the camera. "Sadie, here! I am so pumped to teach you two how to throw and catch a ball! I know little kids like to run around and they're pretty quick. But I'm on the track team. Don't think you can get away from me!"

Finally, it was Delaney's turn. "So there you have it, Baby Noonan 1 and Baby Noonan 2. I'm gonna call you that, since Mom and Dad don't have any names for you yet. I just want you to know I've been practicing a lot and

I'm ready to be your big sister. Actually, I'm really looking forward to meeting you—even if I'm a little scared. But I want you to know I will do my very best. Truly. I even have your first bedtime story all picked out for you." She held up a copy of *Charlotte's Web*.

Delaney hit the button to stop recording. "I think that's a wrap. All I need to do now is add a cool sound track…"

"Of course you do," Kylie said. "That's our Delaney!"

13

Special Delivery

As the red velvet curtains rose on the auditorium stage, the characters of *Charlotte's Web* appeared to leap off the pages of the book (thanks to Lexi's amazing set!) and spring to life. Olivia flapped her feathered arms and honked; Harrison—dressed in a black leather jacket and sunglasses—did his creepiest rat crawl. An assortment of geese, cows, lambs, and even two kids playing the back and front of a horse made their way onstage.

"Where's Delaney?" Sadie whispered to Kylie in the audience. "Isn't she supposed to be on the farm?" All of the cupcake club were there to see Delaney star as Wilbur—even Juliette and her fiancé Rodney.

"I'm not sure I would have directed it this way," he said.

"Shhh!" Juliette hushed him. "This is not Shakespeare and you're not the director. Delaney is!"

Kylie looked around, but there was no pink pig in sight. "I'm sure she'll make a grand entrance."

Of course, she was right. Delaney burst onto the stage with an "Oink!" and did a cartwheel. She wore a pink shirt and leggings, with a curly tail attached at her waist and her pink pig ears perched on her head.

"Will anybody be my friend?" she asked the barnyard animals hopefully before launching into a perky tap-dance routine.

"A friend is someone to play with, to stay with, to dream with, to scheme with…" Delaney sang.

Mr. and Mrs. Noonan were seated in the front row and beamed with pride.

"She's great!" Kylie said, applauding.

Suddenly, Sophie's voice boomed over the loudspeaker. "Salutations, Wilbur! I'll be your friend. Go to sleep now, and in the morning, I'll show you who I am."

"Lights down! Cue the curtain!" Ms. Kutchen called from the wings.

The lights dimmed, and everyone raced offstage to get ready for Charlotte's web-weaving scene.

"Remember, no worries. We got you covered," Tyler assured Sophie.

Corey held up his hands: he was wearing his dad's no-slip work gloves. "Okay, here goes…" Sophie said. As the lights came back up, a web of silvery thread was draped across the proscenium.

"Wait 'til they see your entrance," Delaney whispered, giving her friend a tiny push into the center of the stage.

"I am Charlotte, and this is my web," Sophie said softly. As the music began to play, Tyler and Corey tugged on the rope and she gently rose in the air. She did a beautiful aero-ballet routine, twirling and swirling, high above the stage.

"Oh!" came a loud voice from the audience.

"Wow," Harrison whispered in the wings. "Someone really likes this number."

"Oh! Oh!" came the voice again. Delaney knew that voice. It was her mom!

"Oh! I think it's time!" Mrs. Noonan moaned.

Delaney ran over to Ms. Kutchen. "Stop the show! My mom is in labor!" The house lights went up, and the show came to a screeching halt. Delaney ran into the audience. A crowd was already gathered around her mom.

"It's okay, Laney," her mother assured her. "The babies are just getting ready to make their grand entrance."

"What? Now? It's too early! I'm not ready!" Delaney cried.

"Well, they apparently are." Her mom tried to smile. "Dad's going to take me to the hospital, and Sophie's mom will bring you there after the performance."

Delaney's head was spinning. "Wait! No! I'm going with you!"

Her mother took her hand. "Honey, I'll be fine. You know better than I do that the show must go on. Wilbur can't walk out."

"But, Mommy…" Delaney's eyes filled with tears. "You'll miss it."

"I'll record the whole thing so she can watch it later," Sophie's dad volunteered.

"And I'll take good care of Mommy." Delaney's dad winked. "Trust me, I've been through this before. You were four weeks early yourself. Impatience must run in the Noonan family."

"Oh!" Mrs. Noonan groaned again. "I think we should get going…*now*!"

Ms. Kutchen clapped her hands and summoned everyone's attention. "Please, everybody, take your seats, and, actors, take your places."

Delaney couldn't move. She watched helplessly as her dad and mom made their way out of the auditorium. Her mom was hunched over and panting. She looked like she was in so much pain! Delaney just wanted to run after her!

"Laney, everyone's waiting for you," Kylie said, tapping her friend gently on the shoulder.

Delaney spun around. "I can't. I can't do it. How am I supposed to go up there and sing and dance when my mom is on her way to the hospital?"

"Without you, there's no show," Lexi reminded her.

Kylie nodded. "You have to be strong. I know you're scared, but we're right here for you."

"And where there's a Wilbur, there's a way," Jenna joked, trying to cheer her up.

The girls escorted Delaney up the steps of the stage and behind the curtain where her classmates were all waiting. Sophie looked frantic.

"I thought you were going to leave," she said. "How can I be Charlotte if you're not Wilbur?"

"I'll stay, I guess," Delaney said quietly. Although it was the last thing in the world she felt like doing.

"Thank goodness!" Ms. Kutchen said, dotting her

forehead with a handkerchief. "Show business is so much more complicated than teaching literature!"

She took Delaney by the shoulders and stared into her eyes. "We're counting on you, Delaney," Ms. Kutchen said, giving her a pep talk. "Please don't let me—I mean, us—down."

"I hope you don't mind…I brought someone backstage to say hello." Delaney looked up and saw Ms. Roveen in the wings. Milly was holding her hand and pulling them in Delaney's direction.

"Dee-lay-nee is a piggy!" The little girl giggled. "Oink! Oink!"

Delaney took a deep breath and tried to put on a brave face. "Hi, Milly! Are you watching the show?"

"We are," Ms. Roveen said. "We're loving it, and we're hoping to see the rest."

Milly's head bobbed up and down. "More! More piggy show!" She giggled.

Delaney kneeled down so she could be snout to nose with Milly.

"Okay, Princess Milly, I'll do it for you," she said. "You go back to your seat with Mommy, okay?"

Milly nodded, and Delaney watched as she and Ms. Roveen settled back into their seats.

"The show will now resume," Ms. Kutchen announced over the loudspeaker. Then she added, "I hope... Cue the curtain!"

It was time for the big county-fair scene. Wilbur had to hold his head high and dance around his pen as the entire cast sang, "Oh, gee, what do you see? Zuckerman's Famous Pig!" Delaney closed her eyes and tried to focus. She thought about how proud her parents would be, and how much Milly would enjoy seeing her prance around the stage. She wiggled her tail; she tapped her hooves; she even climbed up on the pen fence and walked across it like a balance beam. When the number was done, she landed in a split and confetti showered down all over the audience.

The crowd went wild. "Great job, Delaney!" Ms. Kutchen told her. "Hang in there!"

The final scene of the show was the saddest: Charlotte was dead, and Wilbur was all alone, waiting for her spider eggs to hatch.

"Wait! Come back!" Delaney cried as the baby spiders blew away in the wind. Then she noticed three little spiders hanging from the barn door.

"Salutations!" came a small voice over the loudspeaker. "We like you...and we like this place. Can we stay?"

Delaney faced the audience and took a deep breath. She knew she was supposed to be Wilbur speaking to Charlotte's babies. But it felt like she was speaking to her own soon-to-be baby brother and sister. "I will love you dearly, forever and ever."

The music swelled, and the entire cast of characters appeared onstage. It was the grand finale that Delaney and Sophie had written!

"It's not every day you find a friend who's with you 'til the very end…" the chorus sang.

Sophie once again swung across the stage, spinning her silver web.

"I'll never forget you," Delaney called to her. "It's not often that someone comes along who's a true friend and a good writer. Charlotte was both…"

With that, the audience sprang to their feet, giving the musical a standing ovation. Milly was standing on her seat, waving and clapping.

Normally Delaney loved the applause and would have come back for several curtain calls. But this time, all she allowed herself was a quick bow before she grabbed Sophie's hand. "Gotta go! Tell your parents we have to get to the hospital! I'm not missing my baby brother and sister being born!"

14

Baby 1 and Baby 2

Delaney paced the floor of the waiting room anxiously. It had been over three hours since her mother went into labor. Where were those babies, and what was taking them so long?

"You're going to wear a hole in the carpet," Sophie's mom Lisa cautioned her. "Don't you want to sit down, Delaney? I can get you a snack from the cafeteria."

"Thanks, but I'm too nervous to eat anything," she replied.

"Even cupcakes?" said a voice from down the hall. It was Kylie, with Jenna, Sadie, and Lexi—and they were carrying a box with them.

"We were saving these to give you after the show," Kylie explained. "But you ran off before we could even say congrats."

Lexi opened the lid. Inside were dark chocolate cupcakes topped with a cream cheese frosting—Delaney's favorite type of cupcake. On top, Lexi had drizzled a chocolate spiderweb.

"That is so cool!" Sophie exclaimed. "If she won't eat one, I will."

"Save me one for later," Delaney said. She was too distracted. "I just wish I knew what was happening."

Finally, a doctor in blue scrubs came to find them. "Hmm, I was told to talk to the pig…" she said.

Delaney's hand shot up. "That's me!"

The doctor chuckled. "Yes, I can see that. The ears gave you away. My name is Dr. Hayem, and I'm your mom's doctor. Would you like to go meet your baby brother and sister?"

Delaney could barely contain her excitement. "You mean they're here?"

Dr. Hayem nodded. "Yes, and I think they're very eager to meet you."

Delaney practically skipped down the hall of the maternity wing and into her mother's room. There, swaddled in one blue and one pink blanket, were her new siblings.

"Oh, my gosh! They're so pretty!" she said. "And perfect!"

"Your brother, Tristan, prefers to be called handsome," her dad said, smiling. "We named him after your great grandpa Truman."

"Do you want to hold him?" her mother asked. She looked exhausted but overjoyed.

"He's light as a feather!" Delaney said, cuddling the tiny baby in her arms. "Hello, little Tristan. Do you know who I am? I'm Delaney, your big sister."

"We don't have a name for your little sister yet," her father said. "We were hoping you could come up with one."

The baby fussed in her mother's arms and began to wail.

"She's going to be a singer like her big sis," her father said. "Just listen to those lungs!"

He took Tristan from her and handed her the pink bundle.

"Don't cry, little girl," Delaney cooed. "I'm here." The infant instantly calmed and opened her blue eyes to look at Delaney.

"Oh, honey, she loves you!" her mom exclaimed.

"I love her too. And I know exactly what we can name her: Charlotte."

Her parents looked at each other and smiled.

"That's perfect," her mom said softly. "Charlotte is a beautiful name—for a spider as well as a baby."

"Tristan and Charlotte Noonan it is," her father

announced. "You think you can forgive them for stealing your spotlight today?"

Delaney planted a tiny kiss on Charlotte's forehead. "Oh, that's okay," she said. "There will be lots of other musicals. It's not every day you get to be a big sister."

☆ ☮ ☆

After a week at home with the twins, Delaney learned first-hand what it was like to be a big sister. She had to admit things were never quite the same. In fact, they were much better! Yes, the babies woke everyone up at 2 a.m. to be fed and needed their diapers changed *all* the time. But every time Tristan or Charlotte cried, the Noonans had their secret weapon!

"Laney, the babies are fussing. Could you please..." her frazzled mom said, testing a baby bottle of warm formula on the back of her wrist.

"Not a prob!" Delaney called, racing into the nursery. Tristan and Charlotte were all red-faced and sobbing.

"Aw, don't cry, Laney's here!" she said, picking up a baby in each arm. "So what will it be today? Beyoncé or Britney?" Charlotte wailed louder. "Britney it is!"

She placed the babies delicately back into their cribs,

tucked them in their blankets, and hit the button on the MP3 player her dad had installed in the nursery.

The beat started to pound as Delaney danced around the room. "Oh, baby, baby, how was I supposed to know?" she belted. "That something wasn't right here?"

By the time she had finished the song, both infants were sleeping soundly. Her mother stood in the doorway smiling. "You have a gift with babies, that's for sure," she said. "I must have sung 'Rock-a-Bye Baby' all night, and I couldn't get them to settle down."

Delaney shrugged. "They just share my taste in music," she said. "Charlotte loves Britney, but Tristan is partial to Maroon 5. 'Moves Like Jagger' knocks him out every time."

Mrs. Noonan nodded her head. "Thanks for the advice, but I think what they're both partial to is their big sister." She kissed Delaney on the top of her head. "Did I ever tell you how amazing you are?"

Delaney rolled her eyes. "Like, every day. But it's okay… you can say it again." She shook her hips, wiggled her butt, and did her best Gaga impression: "I live for the applause, applause, applause…"

Tristan let out a loud burp. "Well," her mom laughed. "I think you just got a burping ovation!"

Delaney smiled. Not even a stadium full of cheering fans chanting her name could have meant more to her. She leaned over the crib and whispered, "If you think that's impressive, just wait 'til you guys can taste my cupcakes."

Princess Milly's Applesauce Cupcakes

The cinnamon in the batter gives these sweet cupcakes a little spice—which is really nice!

For the cupcakes:

- 1 ¼ cups sugar
- 1 ½ cups applesauce
- ½ cup butter (1 stick), softened to room temperature
- 2 eggs
- 2 ½ cups all-purpose flour
- 1 teaspoon ground cinnamon
- 1 teaspoon baking powder
- ½ teaspoon baking soda
- ½ teaspoon salt

Directions

1. Have a grown-up help you preheat the oven to 350°F.

2. Line 24 regular-size muffin cups with cupcake liners. (Pink and princessy ones would be great!)

3. In a large mixing bowl, beat the sugar, applesauce, butter, and eggs on medium speed until the mixture is smooth.

4. Next, on low speed, beat in the flour, cinnamon, baking powder, baking soda, and salt.

5. Fill the liners two-thirds full.

6. Bake approximately 25 minutes or until toothpick inserted in center comes out clean.

7. Cool and frost.

For the vanilla frosting:

½ cup butter (1 stick)

4 cups confectioners' sugar

1 teaspoons vanilla

4 tablespoons milk

Directions

1. In a mixing bowl, combine the butter, confectioners' sugar, and vanilla on medium speed.

2. Slowly add the milk, one tablespoon at a time. (You can add a little more if the frosting seems too thick.)

3. Continue mixing on medium to high speed until the frosting is light and fluffy.

4. If you want, you can add a few drops of food coloring to turn it pink, purple, or powder blue.

5. Decorate with sprinkles, Cheerios, glass slippers… anything your heart desires!

Laffy Taffy Lemonade Cupcakes

These zingy and springy cupcakes are great to serve for brunch, lunch, or even a backyard BBQ!

For the cupcakes:

½ cup (1 stick) unsalted butter, softened to room temperature

1 cup sugar

2 eggs

2 teaspoons vanilla extract

1 ½ cups all-purpose flour

2 teaspoons baking powder

½ teaspoon salt

½ cup milk

Zest and juice of two lemons

Directions

1. Have an adult preheat the oven to 350°F. Line a muffin tin with cupcake liners.

2. In the bowl of an electric mixer, beat the butter and sugar together on medium speed until creamed. (The mixture should be light and fluffy.) Add the eggs and the vanilla, and beat on medium until combined.

3. In a medium-sized bowl, toss together the flour, baking powder, and salt.

4. Slowly add the dry ingredients to the wet ingredients, mixing on low speed.

5. Now add the milk, lemon zest, and lemon juice. Mix until just combined; try not to overmix!

6. Fill the cupcake liners two-thirds full with the batter. I like to use an ice-cream scoop to get the perfect amount.

7. Bake for about 20 minutes or until a toothpick inserted in the middle comes out clean.

8. Cool before frosting.

For the Laffy Taffy Frosting:

10 pieces of fun-size lemon Laffy Taffy

2 tablespoons milk

½ cup butter (1 stick)

1 ½ cups confectioners' sugar

½ tablespoon Vanilla

½ teaspoon yellow food coloring

Directions

1. Since this involves cooking on a stove top, ask an adult for help!

2. Spray your saucepan with nonstick cooking spray.

3. Unwrap the Laffy Taffy pieces and combine with 1 tablespoon of milk over a high flame. Let it melt and simmer, turning the flame down to low.

4. Combine butter and confectioners' sugar in the large bowl of an electric mixer. Add 1 tablespoon of milk and beat.

5. Add the melted Laffy Taffy mixture and the vanilla.

6. If frosting is too thin, slowly add up to ½ cup more confectioners' sugar.

7. Add food coloring to give your frosting a sunny color!

8. After you ice your cupcakes, you can top with an extra piece of Laffy Taffy! Or, if you are having a baby shower, decorate with a mini rubber ducky. (Just don't eat it!)

Delaney's Chocolate Spiderweb Cupcakes

Whether you're a *Charlotte's Web* fan or just want a cool cupcake to serve for Halloween (or any time!), these are *some cupcakes*!

For the cupcakes:

1 ½ cups all-purpose flour

⅔ cup cocoa powder

1 teaspoon baking soda

½ teaspoon salt

1 ½ cups granulated sugar

½ cup (1 stick) butter or margarine, softened

2 large eggs

1 teaspoon vanilla extract

1 cup milk

Directions

1. Have an adult preheat the oven to 350°F. Line a muffin tin with cupcake liners.

2. Mix the flour, cocoa powder, baking soda, and salt together in a medium bowl.

3. In the large bowl of an electric mixer, beat the sugar, butter, eggs, and vanilla.

4. Slowly beat in the flour mixture, alternating with the milk.

5. When all combined, fill liners two-thirds full with batter and bake 18 to 20 minutes (or until wooden toothpick comes out clean).

6. Let cool before frosting.

For the Cream Cheese Frosting:

½ cup of butter (1 stick), softened at room temperature

8 ounces of cream cheese (1 package), softened at room temperature

1 teaspoon vanilla extract

3 cups confectioners' sugar

Directions

1. In the large bowl of an electric mixer, mix the butter

and cream cheese together (about 2 to 3 minutes) on medium speed until smooth. Scrape down the sides and bottom of the bowl to make sure the mixture is well-combined.

2. Add the vanilla extract and mix.

3. Now slowly add the confectioners' sugar. I like to taste to make sure the frosting isn't too sweet before adding a full three cups.

4. Beat until the frosting is creamy smooth.

To create your spider's web...

It looks super-cool, and it's super easy! All you need is some black piping gel and a toothpick.

1. Frost your cupcake first—you can always color the cream-cheese frosting purple, green, or orange for Halloween with some food coloring.

2. Using the black decorating gel, pipe four concentric circles over the top of the cupcake. FYI, this is a small circle that starts in the middle of the cupcake. Make a larger circle around it; then a larger circle around that one and so on until you reach the edge of the cupcake. I do about four or five circles on mine.

3. Now take a toothpick, and carefully drag it from the

center of the cupcake outward, so that the gel gets carried outward to create a cool spiderweb effect. That's it!

Carrie's Tips for Adding "Surprise!" to Your Cupcakes

I love the idea of gender-reveal cupcakes to let everyone know if you're having a baby girl or boy. I first learned about it from my friends Sophie and Katherine who own Georgetown Cupcake and star on *DC Cupcakes* on TV. Katherine revealed she was having a girl by serving her shower guests pink-cream-filled cupcakes. But that's not the only surprise you can add to a cupcake! I admit it: I like to keep my friends and family guessing...

A Cupcake Inside a Cupcake

How cool would it be to bite into a chocolatey cupcake and discover a mini vanilla one inside? Simply bake the inner cupcake first. I like to bake a flat cake in a sheet pan, then use a round or heart-shaped cookie cutter to cut out a "mini" cake. When you are filling your cupcake liner with batter, only fill it halfway. Place the mini inside the batter, then cover with more batter on top. Bake for about 20 minutes. This is a great trick to use for Valentine's Day! You can put red heart shapes smack in the middle of your cupcakes!

Go with the Flow!

After your cupcake is cooled and baked, use an apple corer or a butter knife to cut out the center of the cupcake. Fill with pudding, caramel, marshmallow fluff, fudge, fruit preserves, or anything that has a gooey or oozey texture. Now frost and "cover up" your surprise. When you bite into it, the filling will pour out!

A Sweet Treat

I like to bake my friends' and family's fave mini candy bars right into the center of a cupcake. Dad's is a peanut butter cup or a mini Snickers, but Mom and I prefer Twix! I've even done a rainbow marzipan cookie inside—colorful and cool, don't ya think?

Mix It Up

I like to add texture to my cupcakes, so I'll mash up candy bars, cookies, even bananas, and add them right into the batter.

Whip It Up!

Instead of plain frosting, try something a little lighter—like fresh whipped cream or meringue. It really lets the flavor of the cupcake shine through, especially if it's rich and chocolaty.

Serve It Up!

Instead of an ordinary dinner, serve your family something hearty and savory baked in a cupcake pan! I've done baked ziti cupcakes, spaghetti and meatballs, even meatloaf topped with mashed potato frosting. Simply bake your meatloaf or meatball recipe in a muffin pan (spray with non-stick cooking spray first so it slips out easy), then top with "mashies" and a little gravy. Yum!

It's no secret that I like to bake, and I have a *huge* collection of cupcake recipes to rival even Kylie's! I'm always on the lookout for something fun and new—and I found it in Megan Seling's book and blog (*Bake it in a Cupcake: 50 Treats with a Surprise Inside*; www.bakeitinacake.com)! Basically, there is nothing this woman is afraid to put in the middle of a cupcake, and I love that element of surprise and adventure! I asked her to chat…

Carrie: Why is it cool to add an element of surprise to a cupcake?

Megan: Cupcakes are so great on their own—they're practically the perfect dessert—but the inside of the cupcake has always felt a little empty to me. The bottom of the cupcake is the perfect size and shape to hold a piece of candy, a miniature pie, or a brownie bite, so why not hide something in there? People get really happy when they take a bite and discover that their cupcake is holding a secret treat—it's like getting a second dessert!

Carrie: What is the *weirdest* thing you have ever baked in a cupcake?

Megan: Oh, man, I have had a lot of weird baking experiments. I tried to put Dr Pepper and jelly beans in cupcakes, and that just tasted gross. And while I love gummy worms and Starburst candy, they don't really work in a cupcake, unfortunately. When you bake them into a cupcake, they turn into gross, sticky puddles of goo. The sugary candy just melts and sinks to the bottom, and all the colors blend together and everything turns a greenish brown. Eww! I definitely wasn't expecting that. It took forever to soak the burned sugar bits off my cupcake pan. I've also baked mini marzipan brains into cupcakes. They taste great, but some people get really creeped out by the idea of biting into a brain…even if it is candy.

Carrie: How many cupcakes have you made over the years? What have been your faves?

Megan: I have baked a *lot* of cupcakes—I'm sure I've baked thousands over the years. My absolute favorite is the pumpkin-pie-stuffed cupcake. Pumpkin pie is one of my favorite desserts, and the creamy texture of a pumpkin pie works really well with the texture of the cake. I also really like the lemon-bar-stuffed cupcakes—they taste like lemonade!

Carrie: How can kids learn to be amazing cupcake bakers?

Megan: The most important rule: don't be afraid to experiment! Sometimes the best and only way to know if your idea will work is to try it. And if it's a disaster, that's okay too! Not everything you bake will turn out how you expect it, and that certainly doesn't mean you're a bad baker. Just move on to the next idea. The first time I baked a mini pie into a cupcake, I didn't think it was going to work, but it did! And it was delicious.

Also, practice really does help. When I started baking cupcakes, I was really quite bad at frosting them—I didn't know how to use a pastry bag, and all my cupcakes looked kind of goofy and sloppy. But I practiced with different kinds of decorations and I got better at it, so don't get discouraged when you first start out. As you bake and make things, you'll learn what you're good at and be able to bring your own flare to your creations.

Carrie: What's the secret to a delicious cupcake? What are the elements it must have?

Megan: Butter! Butter definitely helps make really delicious cupcakes. But the thing I really love about cupcakes is that there are no rules. You can have a cupcake with chocolate glaze instead of frosting. You can make cupcakes in different shapes like square or heart shaped, or you can even serve a cupcake upside down!

Carrie: Why are cupcakes cooler than any other dessert? Even cronuts and macaroons!

Megan: Cupcakes are so great because they can be as easy or as fancy as you want them to be. If you don't have much time, whip up a batch of basic cupcakes with a box mix, or if you're feeling a little more adventurous, make the batter from scratch and throw in some experimental ingredients. You can keep things simple and frost them with a traditional swirl of vanilla frosting, or you can get crazy and use all kinds of sprinkles, fondant, and other decorations. Cupcakes are so versatile. Which isn't to say cronuts and macaroons aren't good too—in fact, maybe you should try to bake them into a cupcake!

Here's a sneak peak at the next book in The Cupcake Club series!

Royal Icing

The lobby concierge at The Savoy Hotel handed Kylie a large envelope. "For you, miss," he said. "It was just delivered."

Juliette raised an eyebrow. "Are you sure? Kylie, who would send you a letter all the way here in London?"

Kylie held the large cream-colored envelope up to the twinkly chandelier on the ceiling, trying to see inside. "I have no idea."

Sadie peered over her shoulder. "It looks very fancy," she said. There was gold wax seal on the back, stamped with some sort of Coat of Arms. And it was addressed in a swirly calligraphy script to "The Cupcake Club."

"OMG, do you think it's from Buckingham Palace?" Delaney asked. "That would be so...how do they say 'awesome' again here in London?"

"Brill!" Kylie exclaimed. "As in brilliant."

"Right! That would be brill!" Delaney replied.

"Maybe Prince William and Princess Kate need some cupcakes? Or maybe the Queen has a craving for our *royal* icing!"

Jenna shook her head. "All the way here in England? *No es posible!*"

Kylie smiled. "If there's one thing I've learned after all our cupcake adventures so far, it's that *anything* is possible!" She took a deep breath before tearing into the envelope and pulling out the card inside.

"What does it say?" Lexi asked excitedly. "Is it from the Queen?"

"Or Prince Wills?" Sadie asked. "Maybe he needs cupcakes for his polo match?"

Kylie wasn't listening. She was too engrossed in the letter.

"Kylie, we're dying of suspense," Delaney pleaded with her. "Who's it from? What does it say?"

Kylie cleared her throat and read aloud in her most proper British accent:

"The honour of your presence is hereby requested at a tea hosted by Lord and Lady Wakefield of Wilshire."

Jenna grabbed the card out of her hand. "It's gotta be a practical joke. Someone's pulling our leg."

Juliette nodded. "I'm afraid I've never heard of a Lord

or Lady Wakefield," she said. "Maybe it was meant for someone else."

"I assure you it was intended for you," said a voice behind them. It was a tall man in a long black coat. "I am the attaché to Lord Wakefield."

"What's an attaché?" Delaney whispered.

Kylie shrugged. "I thought it was a briefcase my dad carried to work."

"Archibald Thomas Watson at your service," he said, formally extending his hand to Kylie. "I believe you call it a personal assistant in the States?"

"Oh, yeah!" Delaney interrupted. "All the celebs have personal assistants. The Lord and Lady must be VIPs."

"Indeed," he replied. "And they are planning a very important party that they would like you to bake for. You come highly recommended."

Juliette was suspicious. "Really? By whom? We don't know anyone here in London."

"Oh, but you do," he insisted. "You see, my mate from University told me all about you."

Juliette's eyes grew wide. "Wait a minute...are you...*Archie?*"

The man bowed deeply. "None other."

Juliette threw her arms around him. "It's so wonderful to finally meet you! Rodney said you'd be coming!"

"Okay…you lost me," Jenna sighed. "Who's Archie, and why is Juliette hugging him?"

"Girls, I'd like you to meet Rodney's college BFF Archie," she said, smiling. "Oh, I've heard so much about you!"

Archie blushed. "Only good things, I hope. Rodney didn't tell you the fish and chips story did he? I swear, I didn't mean to get one stuck in his ear. It was all in good fun!"

Suddenly the pieces started to come together. It was Juliette's fiancé who had recommended them!

"Excuse me?" Kylie said, raising her hand. "It's very nice to meet you, Archie. But you still haven't told us what you want Peace, Love and Cupcakes to do." They had arrived only a few days ago in the UK at Juliette's invitation to see Rodney open in *Macbeth* on The West End. She knew her friends wanted to go on the Harry Potter tour of London and check out Hummingbird Bakery in Notting Hill today. Out of the corner of her eye she could see Sadie making the "time out" sign with her hands. But a party for a lord and lady was tough to turn down…

"Kylie, remember we have plans," Sadie interrupted her. "I am not leaving London until I visit Wembley Stadium."

Archie smiled. "The party is Sunday, and today's only Tuesday. That leaves you plenty of time to make 500 cupcakes for their guests *and* get in your sightseeing."

Kylie pulled out her notebook from her backpack and started jotting. "Okay, 500 cupcakes should be doable if we get started recipe testing tomorrow."

"Kylie," Jenna reminded her. "We said we were going to Harrods's Food Hall tomorrow. I have an entire list of truffles I need to try."

"And to The National Gallery Thursday," Lexi added. "Remember? Van Gogh's two Sunflower Paintings are there together for the first time in 65 years?"

"I dunno," Delaney shrugged. "A fancy tea party sounds like a lot more fun than some old art exhibit, a soccer stadium, or a department store."

Kylie was glad to hear at least *someone* was on her side! "Look, guys. Let's hear Archie out. I'm sure we can make time to do it all," Kylie pleaded.

"Fine," Lexi agreed. "Where's this party? And do we even have a kitchen to bake in?"

"You are welcome to use the kitchen in the Wakefield estate. It's large with all the equipment you'll need."

Kylie chewed her pencil eraser. "Chocolate frosting? Vanilla?"

"I believe Lady Lillianne is partial to Curly Wurly," Archie replied.

"Who is Lady Lillianne?" Sadie asked.

"And more importantly—what the heck is a Curly Wurly?" Delaney added.

"Lady Lillianne is Lord and Lady Wakefield's daughter, and the tea is in honor of her thirteenth birthday."

"And a Curly Wurly is a candy bar here in London, "Jenna piped up. "I tried one the other day at The Tube station. Chocolate covered caramel in this twisty shape. It kinda looks like a ladder."

"Precisely!" Archie replied. "Which should be perfect for the architectural structure."

This time it was Lexi's turn to raise her hand. "Excuse me, I'm the artist. What architectural structure?" She tore a sheet out of Kylie's notebook, preparing to sketch.

"Ah, yes, sorry, I forgot to mention the display for your cupcakes," Archie apologized. "It's a bit complicated…"

"I have a bad feeling about this," Lexi whispered.

"You see, her ladyship would like a London Bridge… made out of cupcakes."

Lexi gasped. "As in London Bridge is falling down?"

"Precisely," Archie smiled. "The tea is to be held in the North Tower Lounge of the Bridge."

Kylie was already flipping through her Fodor's Guide Book to London. "The London Tower Bridge spans across the Thames River," she read aloud. "It's a bascule bridge—which is French for the word 'see-saw.'"

Lexi nodded. "As in up and down since the bottom of the bridge goes up and down." She quickly drew a picture of a bridge opened and a boat sailing through the river. "I could do blue gel icing for the water."

"There are two towers on either side and a huge walkway between them," Kylie continued.

"How huge are we talking?" Sadie asked. "Because my dad's contracting shop is all the way back home in New Fairfield." She turned to Archie. "We're bakers, not builders."

"Hey, you're talking to the Queen of Legos," Jenna volunteered. "My little brothers Ricky and Manny are always building bridges. I got this."

"Whatever you need, I'm at your service," Archie replied. "Flour, sugar, baking tins."

Lexi did some quick math and handed him a sheet of paper. "Let's start with this: five hundred Curly Wurly

Bars and fifty cans of Meringue Powder. That should be enough for a five-foot long display, I think."

Archie scratched his head. "What will you do with all that powder?"

Kylie smiled. "We're going to gumpaste-glue you a London Bridge that will knock your socks off!"

Archie stared down at his socks. "Yes, well, it's rather chilly today so I like my socks where they are."

Juliette laughed. "What Kylie means is please tell Lord and Lady Wakefield that we're going to make their daughter a wonderful cupcake bridge for her birthday."

Archie looked relieved. "Very well, then. Here is the address of the Wakefield estate. You're welcome to begin straight away." He handed Juliette his calling card.

"Pip, pip, cheerio!" Delaney said, waving goodbye as Archie strolled out of the hotel.

"I think someone has seen Mary Poppins one too many times," Jenna teased her.

"I'm just trying to speak the language," Delaney insisted.

It was fun to hang out in the hotel lobby listening to the locals and lounging on the plush velvet couches, but Kylie didn't want to waste another second. "I think we should decide on the cupcake flavors—something that would work for a British tea."

"How about bangers and mash?" Delaney volunteered. "A sausage and mashed potato cupcake?"

Jenna wrinkled her nose. "Next!"

"Let's do a Curly Wurly-inspired cupcake," Sadie suggested. "Chocolate and caramel together."

"Prestat is the Queen's official chocolatier," Jenna pointed out. "And they do this amazing milk chocolate with Earl Grey tea in it."

"Did anyone ever tell you that you are an encyclopedia of sweets?" Sadie marveled.

"A chocolate Earl Grey tea cupcake it is," Kylie said.

"And we can make a rich caramel frosting with dark brown sugar," Lexi suggested. She looked at the picture of the bridge in Kylie's tour book. "It's kind of silvery-gray, light blue and white. I can do fondant circles in those three colors and give it a bit of metallic shimmer with edible glitter."

"Then what are we waiting for?" Kylie asked. "Let's hit Covent Garden market first, then head to Prestat on Piccadilly for the chocolate. She marked all the points on her map of London with a red star. "Spit spot!"

Acknowledgments

To all our new friends, teachers, and advisors at Trevor: love you guys! You have embraced us with open arms and made us feel so welcome! Couldn't ask for a more amazing school to inspire the next chapters in The Cupcake Club series—have fun with your "shout-outs" in this book! Skylar and Sophie, Carrie's TDS besties: you guys are what great friends are all about! MWAH! Olivia, Yael, Harrison, Casey, Gabby, Rhiannon...you're now officially in a book! Ms. Robine: thanks for being such a great advisor! *Merci!* Ms. Hutchin: thanks for inspiring kids to be great readers/writers! Maybe a *Charlotte's Web* musical for next mini term?

Delaney and the Hannons: we miss you! Thanks for all the great times we had at PS 6. Delaney, your sparkle and fun truly inspired this character. This one's for you!

Hugs and sprinkles to Emily/Terrence Noonan; the Goldstein Girls, Sadie and Lila, Jamie Ludwig, the BAE

Level 4 and 5 friends (Julia I.: did you find your shout-out?). And of course, Darby Dutter—Carrie's very first BFF. Your Jekyll and Hyde party this year was great inspiration for all of Delaney and Kylie's monster mania scenes! And your friendship is always the model for the PLC girls sticking together through thick and thin!

Holly, Kathy, Stacy, Deb, Mish: as always, you are the best friends. When can we have a "Holly-day"?

To Mildred Goldberg, Sheryl's second-grade teacher at PS 24, who told her she could be a great writer. Silly Milly is for you…

To the Berks, Kahns, and Saps: as always, you are our biggest fans! Daddy, we love you to the moon and stars! Maddie: big sloppy puppy kisses!

Katherine and Frank at Folio Lit: you rock! Thanks for always believing in us.

To our team at Sourcebooks Jabberwocky: thanks as always for being so sweet! Hugs and sprinkles to Steve, Derry, Leah, Jillian, and Cat.

A big thanks to Megan Seling for the awesome interview!

About the Authors

Sheryl Berk is the *New York Times* bestselling co-author of *Soul Surfer*. An entertainment editor and journalist, she has written dozens of books with celebrities including Britney Spears, Jenna Ushkowitz, and Zendaya.

Photo credit: Jack Saperstone

Her ten-year-old daughter, Carrie Berk, a cupcake connoisseur and blogger (www.facebook.com/PLCCupcakeClub; www.carriescupakecritique.shutterfly.com), cooked up the idea for The Cupcake Club series while in second grade. To date, they have written five books together (with many more in the works!). *Peace, Love, and Cupcakes* is also slated to be a delicious new musical from New York City's Vital Theatre in 2014.

Peace Love and CUPCAKES

Meet Kylie Carson.

She's a fourth grader with a big problem. How will she make friends at her new school? Should she tell her classmates she loves monster movies? Forget it. Play the part of a turnip in the school play? Disaster! Then Kylie comes up with a delicious idea: What if she starts a cupcake club?

Soon Kylie's club is spinning out tasty treats with the help of her fellow bakers and new friends. But when Meredith tries to sabotage the girls' big cupcake party, will it be the end of the cupcake club?

Book
1

Recipe For Trouble

Meet Lexi Poole.

To Lexi, a new school year means back to baking with her BFFs in the cupcake club. But the club president, Kylie, is mixing things up by inviting new members. And Lexi is in for a not-so-sweet surprise when she is cast in the school's production of *Romeo and Juliet*. If only she could be as confident onstage as she is in the kitchen. The icing on the cake: her secret crush is playing Romeo. Sounds like a recipe for trouble!

Can the girls' friendship stand the heat, or will the cupcake club go up in smoke?

Book
2

Winner Bakes All

$\mathcal{M}$eet Sadie.

When she's not mixing it up on the basketball court, she's mixing the perfect batter with her friends in the cupcake club. Sadie's definitely no stranger to competition, but the oven mitts are off when the club is chosen to appear on *Battle of the Bakers*, the ultimate cupcake competition on TV. If the girls want a taste of sweet victory, they'll have to beat the very best bakers. But the real battle happens off camera when the club's baking business starts losing money. Long recipe short, no money for icing and sprinkles means no cupcake club.

With the clock ticking and the cameras rolling, will the club and their cupcakes rise to the occasion?

Book
3

Icing on the Cake

Meet Jenna.

She's the cupcake club's official taste tester, but the past few weeks have not been so sweet. Her mom just got engaged to Leo—who Jenna is sure is not "The One"—and Peace, Love, and Cupcakes has to bake the wedding cake. Jenna is ready to throw in the towel, especially when she hears the wedding will be in Las Vegas on Easter weekend, one of the most important holidays for the club's business!

Can Jenna and her friends handle their busy orders—and the Elvis impersonators—or will they have a cupcake meltdown?

Book
4

The Cupcake Club Collection

Enjoy the first three books of The Cupcake Club series in one set!

A treasure trove of delicious treats—The Cupcake Club Collection will satisfy any sweet tooth! Get the first three books in this popular new series by *New York Times* bestselling author Sheryl Berk and her cupcake-loving daughter, Carrie. Each book features yummy original recipes from the story, and we've included a special edition recipe card for the best cupcakes yet! Don't miss out on your chance to own the set!